The River
Beneath
The River

The River Beneath The River

A Novel of the Awakening Spirit

Susan Jabin

Clear View Press
Los Angeles ~ California

The River Beneath The River
www.susantabin.com

Copyright © 2004 by Susan Tabin

Published in the United States by
Clear View Press, Inc.
PO Box 11574, Marina del Rey, CA 90295.

This is a work of fiction. All of the characters
and events portrayed in this novel are either
fictitious or are used fictitiously.

Library of Congress Cataloging-in-Publication Data

Tabin, Susan.
   The river beneath the river : a novel of the awakening spirit / Susan Tabin.
      p. cm.
   ISBN 0-9743793-5-2 (trade pbk.)
   1. Young women--Fiction. 2. Women travelers--Fiction. 3. Brooklyn (New
York, N.Y.)--Fiction. 4. Americans--Foreign countries--Fiction. I. Title.
   PS3620.A25R59 2004
813'.6--dc22

                                                2003028171

ISBN 0-9743793-5-2

Cover art by Larry Whittaker
Book design by Robert Aulicino

Printed in the United States of America

0 9 8 7 6 5 4 3 2 1

In loving memory of Helene, my sister,
my forever friend.

Acknowledgments

The great blessing in my life has been the people I have had the privilege of knowing. Thank you to my family and friends. I love you all.

I especially want to thank Mark Penzer for being so generous with his time. His guidance in the craft of writing and his brilliant editing have been invaluable to me. I am grateful to Larry Whittaker for creating the splendid work of art that graces the cover. My thanks also go to Laren Bright whose review and excellent suggestions have enhanced this book.

Heartfelt thanks to my brother, Howard Levine, for listening to me read the first manuscript draft over the phone and for his helpful suggestions. Thank you to my niece, Marcia Sarah Bate, for loving the story and for the box of Darjeeling Tea. Thank you to Eileen Brown, Lin Whittaker, Nydia Rey and Sharon Huff for reading the manuscript and for their feedback, but mostly for their love and support.

Along the writing way there were many well wishers. I particularly want to thank my nephew, Chuck Solomon, and my brother-in-law, John Bate, for research assistance, and to Miriam Goldstein, Greg Nesper and Sherry Funt for their enthusiasm and encouragement.

Finally, I am deeply grateful to my beautiful husband, Ron, for his love and patience; to my Light-filled daughter, Mindy for inputting early chapters into the computer and for her insight; to my amazing son, Brett who made it possible for the manuscript to be brought into this published book form, and always to my spiritual teachers for holding the Light.

He said, "Come to the Edge."

I said. "I can't. I'm afraid."

He said, "Come to the Edge."

I said. "I can't. I'll fall off."

He said, "Come to the Edge."

And I came to the Edge.

And he pushed me.

And I flew.

-Guillaume Apollinaire

Part One

One

I had made love to my brother. Of course I didn't know he was my brother at the time, nor did he. How I got there is a story filled with odd twists which in retrospect don't seem odd at all. What is important about my having made love to my brother is how it unlocked some key for me of understanding that when life presses against me leaving me damaged and gasping for air the measure of my resilience is up to me. *It's my choice.* I didn't spend years in therapy, but I didn't come to this realization on my own either. An extraordinary being named Ere Zeta who I met in Spain and who even today I cannot swear is real or perhaps even human, helped me to heal myself, to accept the unacceptable, and to see life's events on a much grander scale. The cosmic force that lured me kicking and screaming to where I am as I tell my story began, at least in this lifetime, when my parents fell in love over a cup of Darjeeling tea. During her pregnancy my mother's small breasts grew enormous—to a size D. That cinched it, it was preordained that I would have a D name. They called me Darci. I was happy they didn't call me Darjeeling—still I never felt right about my name or about myself. I just didn't belong... in my family, in New York. I didn't fit in.

I didn't fit in with the other teenage girls and when they snubbed me, *I showed them.* The hand-me-down skirt with the pictures of the Queen's coronation, from my cousin May, became a souvenir from my trip to London, where I attended the royal crowning. That's what I told the unfriendly girls.

It was not until later, when I was able to appreciate how my life's course was influenced by inexplicable occurrences beyond my understanding, that I really began to know who I was. But as a child, I didn't feel like I belonged in my own skin. It's white. I wanted to be with the colored people who hung out on the stoops of the aging buildings along Blake Avenue in Brooklyn, where my parents shopped for food in the din of marketplace bustle, amid mounds of vegetables, fruits, hard-shelled nuts and smelly fish hawked by immigrant pushcart vendors.

My parents weren't immigrants, they were born in New York—my mother, Sela, who looked a lot like Lucille Ball, in the Bronx and my father, Pini, who looked a little like Desi Arnaz, in Brooklyn. The resemblances ended there. My parent's life wasn't even remotely funny. The parental world was narrow though not provincial. They were after all liberal Jews, *liberal by the standards of 1951*, when they shopped on Blake Avenue and left me in the old dented black sedan to admire the charlotte russes in the window of Sugarman's Bakery.

One of these I would get if, my mother promised in her soft voice, "You sit and wait like a good girl, Darci."

A cupcake-size, yellow sponge pastry, in a white scalloped cardboard holder, topped with whipped cream and a maraschino cherry. *Oh I wanted it.* I also wanted to be with the dark-skinned, strong-bottomed women who were bumping and grinding and thrusting themselves up against the dark-skinned men who bumped and gyrated and thrusted back, whiskey bottles in brown paper bags in hand. The playful talk, the loose lips, loose hips, the colorful cotton clothing and nappy hair were all inviting to me as chunks of rich chocolate.

When one day my parents returned to the car I asked, "What does fuck mean?"

My mother's long neck turned red and blotchy. My bull-necked, broad shouldered father stiffened like a number 2 pencil. "Darci, you heard that from the *schvartzers*—don't say that. It's a dirty word!"

I didn't get a charlotte russe that day, and I never forgot my introduction to dirty words. For a long time I was under the spell of the strange word that mortified my parents while the dark-skinned grownups verbally had permission to express their impulses, gratify their appetites and be free as birds. For a long time I secretly wanted to say "fuck me" to a dark-skinned man.

The first time I saw a dark-skinned person I was with my father at the Scranton train station. Black as coal. I couldn't take my eyes off him; I didn't want to take my eyes off him. He was the most compelling looking man I'd ever seen. Decades before the "Black is Beautiful" slogan was born, the black train station porter was utterly beautiful to this five-year-old beholder. I was fascinated by the way the man looked, his color, his flat nose, his friendliness when he knelt down to my size and called me "chile," as in, "Here's a piece of candy for you, sweet chile." Everything about the irresistible man seemed vaguely familiar. A sense of recognition was stirring in me, like the primal music of a seashell held close to my ear, coaxing me to recall.

Four years later, at nine, having moved from the honeysuckle scented foothills of northeast Pennsylvania back to Brooklyn, the colored folks on the red paint-peeled stoop in the sticky heat of a New York summer seemed all the more familiar. The stirring in me was the beginning of a longing to know my own heart and the hearts of others.

✻

T John was a cocoa-skinned Negro boy in my third grade class. We were friends. Like a hummingbird's tongue stretched forth to sweet nectar I was drawn to him immediately.

"Rudolph the red nose reindeer—no one has a red nose," T John said, heaving his skinny body into a swell of laughter.

"Why not, T John? You have a brown nose."

T John buried his head in his hands, hiding his face.

"I'm sorry," I said to T John, but there was no taking back the words. Like birds flown the coop, they were out. "I didn't mean to hurt your feelings, T John. I like your color."

"I hate it; the kids say I have doody on me," he said in a muffled whimper as he sat down at his wooden lift-top desk and continued to cover his brown face.

"Darci, I won't be home this afternoon. I have a doctor appointment. Go to Grandma and Papa's after school," my mother had instructed in the morning while she soothingly brushed the sleep out of my dark brown hair and tamed my hair in a ponytail. Her knobby arthritic fingers wrapped around the flat handle of the brush didn't fit with the rest of her body. She was pretty, my mother, with her long swan-neck, high apple-cheeks, and strawberry blond hair.

When the final bell rang, I told T John, "I'm not goin' home today. I'm goin' to Milford Street; it's on the way. I can walk with you."

T John looked down at his mirror-polished shoes, shifted from side to side, shrugged one bony shoulder into a "whatever," and we walked together. T John was tired of being teased about his color. He refused to fully accept my apology and by the end of the school year our wilted friendship had shriveled and liquefied like a virused caterpillar. A parting took place between us, a tugging emotion I would experience again.

People would come in and out of my life in an unpredictable, unsteady procession. For one reason or another, obvious or unrevealed, some left while others were *taken* from me. And some friendships chilled while others ended—sometimes abruptly, sometimes slowly, and sometimes, like the imperceptible receding of a glacier, so subtle, that it was only in looking back I realized a relationship had simply faded away.

Two

Riva and Harry Beriman lived on a slow Brooklyn block crowded with old maple trees and small wood houses. Grandma Riva said the houses were older than the moon. "But," she always quickly added with affection, "Milford's a plum, like a small-town street." I love the way her skin smelled of lavender, and how her little front yard garden was filled with snowball flowers, pink and bluish. Grandma always said, "This garden is impossible, small as a thimble. One of these days the hydrangeas are gonna strangle the lions."

The lions stood like concrete sentries on each side of the three steps to the red frame house. One lion was missing its front paw and the other one, a nose.

"Come sit down, have a glass of milk, Darcilah," Grandma said on a day I recall vividly.

I passed bunches of shiny green, spindly mother-in-law's tongue plants in tall, chipped brown clay urns, and sank into the cushions of a wicker armchair. I could hardly see the yellow and red tulips on the cushions anymore. The stucco walls of the house were the color of the mustard we spread on Hebrew National hot dogs, but the walls were all faded too.

Squinting against the light coming through the bay window, as if she could read my thoughts, Grandma said, "It's a sun porch and the windows should be uncurtained—and that's that."

I finished the cold milk, put my glass down on a low square wicker table with chubby feet and asked, "Grandma, can I play in the cellar?"

"Yes, but be careful on the steps, Darcilah, and stay away from the dresser with Papa's tools."

I held onto the banister and descended the steep creaky stairs. I heard my grandfather, Papa Harry, humming *America The Beautiful.* He put the wood saw down when he saw me and I jumped into his arms. Papa was gray like a cloudy day, and tall and thin with graying hair under a black skull cap that looked like a beanie. His chin was studded with prickly whiskers. Papa was completely different in stature from Grandma who was much shorter, darker and a little bowlegged, with a great soft bosom, round as the whole world. Papa's nose was long, narrow and straight. His neck curved like a Christmas candy cane and every day he walked in a bent over shuffle to the orthodox temple on Atkins Avenue. Sometimes I went with him, but I didn't like having to stay separate from him there. Women and even girls sat up in the balcony away from the praying, swaying men on the main floor.

For me, Papa's basement was the real holy place where I could watch him hammer and saw and make wine by crushing the fat grapes that grew on vines beside the house. The walls in the basement were lined with shelves and the shelves were lined with round Quaker Oatmeal containers filled with nails, screws, nuts and bolts—all kinds of building stuff. Papa's basement looked like an assembly of Quaker men, shoulder to shoulder in their black coats and Quaker hats.

Papa opened the hatch door leading to the ground above. Crisp air and late afternoon light flood in filled with sawdust particles that Grandma Riva says whirl like God-intoxicated Dervishes. The light is funneled in the direction of an old maple dresser. The mysterious dresser that Grandma constantly commands me not to open. I had thought about snooping and I had approached the forbidden bureau once asking if I could look through the drawers, but Grandma had gotten so upset that I never mentioned it again. Besides, I knew it was always kept locked. As I give it my usual glance I notice something different. One of the drawers is not closed all the way. Almost. But not quite. Today like a compass needle pointing north I'm propelled toward it. I'm not sure why or what I'm looking for, but I'm on a mission as I tug at the left side middle drawer, so stuck it seems to be holding its breath, determined not to be opened. I manage to lure it partially out. Reaching inside I rummage through the drawer, feeling some papers and pulling them forward, when Papa calls.

"Darci, *shayne maideleh*," beautiful girl in Yiddish. It didn't matter that Papa spoke Yiddish and Russian and not a word of

English. He talked to me with his watery blue eyes, his faint smile and I knew that he loved me.

Like a wooden bird springing out of a cuckoo clock announcing the hour, I sprang out all wide-eyed in front of Papa to let him know that I was okay and to keep him from checking on me, and I immediately returned to the papers. In my small dusty hands I held a photograph and a marriage license. The photo was of my father with a young braided-haired woman who was not my mother and a little boy standing between them. My father was handsome, younger and thinner, the woman was unfamiliar, and the brown-haired boy in the striped polo shirt was just a toddler. The marriage certificate read Pinchas Theodore Beriman and Mary Alice O'Malley. I stared at the photo, then at the license, back to the photo and again to the license. "What is this? This can't be," I thought aloud. But I also understood, making note of the June 5, 1936 date on the marriage certificate, that whatever this was it took place before Pini, Sela and Darci Beriman. *This was Pini, Mary Alice and another Beriman child.* Where was this child I wondered and my curiosity frightened me. For all I knew he could be as far away as Neptune or Pluto. Or maybe my father had swallowed him like the Roman god Saturn who had swallowed five of his children because an oracle said that one of his children would overthrow him.

How could my family not tell me this? They conveniently edited the book of life and acted as if all this didn't exist. I was shaken to the marrow of my being. I felt weak as if I were made of clay and might crumble. My hands were trembling. I closed my eyelids, sniffed a deep nervous breath and whispered, "Darci Beriman, Y–G–T–T. . . You'll–Get–Through–This."

I felt like a spy as I shoved the marriage license and the ragged edged photograph in as far as I could and pushed the warped drawer back into its dark resting-place. I didn't want to upset my parents so I kept the discovery, like a mouth with a canker sore, to myself. Years later I would rue the day I kept this discovery from my parents. But how could I have known that my father's secret would become my shame.

Three

"Why won't your mother let us live upstairs now that the renters are out?" my mother pleaded again.

Annoyed, my father raised his baritone voice, "Look, for the goddamn hundredth time, Sela, can't you understand, she doesn't want us to move in, she wants the full rent."

With her knobby knuckled fingers clenched in fistfuls of anger, my mother demanded, "We need more room, Pini, even if we don't have the money." Her long neck began to turn blotchy and her pretty face flushed almost to the color of her chin length, wavy strawberry blond hair. She blurted out, "I hate her."

My father screamed louder, "Don't talk about my mother, you idiot."

My mother cried, "You black dog bimbo."

I cringed, holding my hands over my ears and hurried outside.

Whenever my parents argued over money or our cramped quarters, twisting my world into a spastic kaleidoscope of emotions, I fled the apartment for the streets, developing an independence of coming and going that belied my years.

In the Kasbah-like alleyways between the low-rise tenement buildings on our block, under lines of drying laundry, I played punchball, stickball, cowboys and Indians with neighborhood kids. I can almost taste the explosive cracking, the sulfurous scorch of the red cap rolls that we banged away at in our cap guns. And across the alley under a sycamore tree, its leaves flat as my chest, its white bark an immigration history carved with Italian, Irish and Jewish names, we took turns throwing pocket-knives into the ground, drawing lines in the dirt and claiming miniscule slices of territory as our own in a game called "War."

"It's dumb, they call these garden apartments, there aren't any gardens here, just some grass," I complained to my friend Natalie. As the sweet smell of roses wafted across my memory and my senses drifted to a fragrant oasis in the midst of Brooklyn, I explained, "I've been to the Botanic Gardens with my father."

"You're lucky, Dar, your dad takes you so many places."

"I know. The Bronx Zoo, the Empire State Building , the Statue of Liberty."

His dark pompadour rising from his forehead like a tuft of plumes and slicked with pomade, my olive-complexioned father dutifully took me to much of the affordable and free culture New York City had to offer. He was like a different person on those trips. Away from the bleakness of his life at home, just the two of us, he was a real "dad." He was sweet and caring, teaching me about the rich culture he was so proud of. I didn't know my family was poor until I repeatedly begged, "Please, please, Daddy can I get a two-wheeler, please?" and ended up with a hot pink, too many times painted over, second-hand bike. It's shabbiness didn't diminish my enjoyment and it was the only bicycle I had throughout my childhood.

Natalie was my best friend since third grade. She had the friendliest round face with rosy cheeks, soft pale flaxen hair, wonderful eyes shiny and black as marbles in a Chinese checkers game, a button nose and delicate lips that curled at the edges into a permanent smile. She was thin as a potato chip and though we were the same age she was three inches shorter than me. Natalie was daring and zany and I loved her.

Natalie's father, Guy, a deeply tanned, graying at the temples distinguished looking man, worked nights as a waiter in a Manhattan bar and grill. He came home at two in the mornings, his pockets bulging with appreciation. He was always sound asleep, his head beneath two feather pillows, when Natalie awoke at seven o'clock and *pilfered* enough of the small change to keep the two us supplied with gum, miniature wax candy bottles filled with syrup, and charms from the penny machines at the candy store.

Alone at Guy and Jacqueline Palermo's meager two-bedroom apartment one freezing January afternoon, we decided to wash the kitchen floor.

"Let's take our clothes off," Natalie urged, "so we don't get them wet."

That's all it took. We quickly stripped out of our leggings, itchy wool sweaters, brown oxford shoes, socks, undershirts and panties. Twice we filled up a bucket with soapy Spic N Span water; poured it all out onto the small kitchen floor. Buck naked and squealing raucously like seagulls we abandoned reality, mermaids riding the waves at Coney Island beach, we slid back and forth along the saturated split pea soup color linoleum.

"Listen! I hear someone at the door."

"Oh my God, my mother's home," Natalie moaned as she picked up speed and slid right smack into the nest of hot radiator pipes.

Mrs. Palermo, with Anthony, her five-year-old son in tow, dropped the shopping bag filled with groceries, stepped out of her high heel shoes, waded into her immaculate kitchen and screamed, "Mary, mother of Jesus, are you two crazy!"

Natalie couldn't answer. She was crying hysterically from the blistering burn on her bare behind.

Her mother's black eyes grew huge; with her arms lifted to the sides and slightly to the front of her head, her hands were vibrating wildly. She looked as if she might pull her own head off. Her fingernails were painted bright red like ten red crested wood-peckers about to bore holes in me.

Under my breath I began rapidly repeating, "Darci Beriman, Y–G–T–T … Natalie Palermo, Y–G–T–T…You'll–Get–Through–This."

She yelled at me, "Get dressed and go home you little wild animal."

And I was an animal, not a girl, trapped, skinned alive, humiliated and shamefully aware of my nakedness. I wanted to hug Natalie, but I was scared and I obeyed Mrs. Palermo. I dressed in a flash; without looking directly at her I said in my quietest voice, "I'm sorry Mrs. P." I was wet, sudsy and sockless as I walked hurriedly outside into the bitter cold second day of 1953.

When I turned the familiar corner to Liberty, the avenue I lived on, a Christmas tree glistening with the remnants of silver tinsel caught my eye. I forgot the cold and sprinted toward it, assured that it had been put there for that very moment in my life. Without hesitation I lifted the trunk and dragged the dead tree out of the gutter and up two flights of stairs to my family's one-bedroom flat, leaving a trail of pine needles and tinsel in the narrow stairwell.

When she heard me come in through the door, which was usually unlocked during the day, my mother peeked out from the tiny kitchen. Her eyes widened, then she shook her head.

"Darci Ann Beriman, I can't keep up with you!"

"Mom, it's free, it was outside. Isn't it beautiful? Can we put lights on it?"

"What am I gonna do with you, look at this mess," my mother said, half-laughing, half-crying. "We can't keep this! Jews don't have Christmas trees!" she said.

"But, Mom, if we fix it up maybe Santa'll come to our house," I argued.

"Darci, you know Santa Claus isn't a real person. Remember we went to Macy's, you saw a Santa outside, then you saw another inside?"

My eyes puddled up with tears. "Of course I know he isn't a real person, he's a magic person."

My mother let out a sigh, "Darci, Santa Claus is a figment of the Christian imagination. Like Jesus. They're not real."

I wrinkled my nose, did a pouty kind of thing with my lips, raised my eyes heavenward and thought about what my mother had just told me.

"But imagination is good, Mom, that's where everything lives inside of me."

We could hear my father's slow heavy-footed climb up the steps and we turned when he came in the door. He was dirty from his construction job and obviously tired and cold. With the tree and the three of us, the small walk-through living room, which doubled as my parent's bedroom, was overflowing. From where I was standing I could see into every room in our flat, the narrow kitchen to the left, the bathroom and my bedroom to the rear. Except for the bathroom with its dingy white tile small as sugar cubes, the floor throughout the rest of the apartment was covered in green linoleum embellished with rows of green leafy globular shapes. It seemed to me as if we lived in a half-furnished cabbage patch. My father kissed my mother on the cheek, poked at my belly lovingly, shook his head.

"What's goin' on here, we converting?" he asked.

"Your daughter wants to have Christmas," my mother answered.

My father roared with laughter, shaking the apartment. Then quieting into exhaustion, with a grin still on his face, he said,

"Next year maybe we can have a Chanukah bush."

I never knew what to expect from my father. One minute he was angry and gruff; the next minute kind and concerned. The only thing I was sure of was that my father always seemed to be motivated by having to be right. The promise of a tree a year away, the mere possibility had me crossing my fingers behind my back and hoping this wasn't some temporary whim. I stretched my eyes wide open; my pouted lips turned into a toothy grin. My father looked at me for a long time. I have his green almond eyes with the same dark lashes and long narrow straight Beriman nose. My skin is olive oil-smooth like his Greek mother's. I'm willowy and tall like Papa. I have my mother's long neck, her high apple cheeks. My clothing and my religion are also hand-me-downs. *My thoughts are my own.*

"Darci, I'm gonna put the tree back in the street. Help your mother clean up."

I nodded, "I will, Daddy."

But first I bent down, picked up three strands of shiny tinsel, a broken pine branch, and put them in the Buster Brown shoe box anointing my collection of Coney Island shells, rocks, baby teeth, two Long Island duck feathers and one very dead yellow and black zebra heliconian butterfly, its wings fully outspread, with the contraband perfume of Christmas.

Four

Natalie's encounter with the hot radiator and her mother's scalding reprimand didn't deter us from mischievous and sublime adventures over the next year that we both lived in the gardenless garden apartments.

In April, her behind well healed, she asked, "You wanna go to church with me?"

"Yeah, do they have those powdered sugar doughy things?"

"You mean the zeppoles?"

"Yeah, the zeppoles." My mouth watered remembering the taste of the deep fried confections that were sold at the church festival.

"Nuh, there's no food at Saint Catherine's, well, unless you count the bread at Holy Communion."

"Why do they have bread instead of zeppoles?"

Natalie giggled, and rolled her eyes. "The bread is the body of Jesus, and the wine we drink is his blood."

"Yuck, drinking blood." I squinched my nose and closed my almond eyes to mere slivers.

Natalie slid her arm around my waist and I wrapped my arm around hers. We walked toward Saint Catherine's and into a collective remembrance of the festival when the narrow Brooklyn streets lined with makeshift booths came alive, like a constellation of stars against the dark, with strings of lights and the aroma of the best Italian food East New York had to offer. Plump sausages with lush green peppers and sweet onions sautéed in golden olive oil; fried eggs and peppers on fresh baked crusty Italian bread, and thin moist spaghetti strands that we sucked up right out of the thick red tomato sauce.

"What was your favorite booth at the festival?" I asked Nat.

"Coin toss—of course."

I laughed, "Yeah, that was so fun when we licked the nickels, they stuck to the glass dishes."

"Yeah, the nickels didn't bounce out. I won the goldfish, you got the turtle," Natalie remembered.

That little olive turtle no bigger than a quarter, with the bright yellow rose painted on its shell. Myrtle the turtle died after a few weeks, probably from lead poisoning my father thought. He took me to the library. I learned that all turtles hatch from eggs and never know their parents. *I identified with turtles.* I didn't really know my parents with their secret lives, my father with his hushed marriage and hidden child.

I pulled Natalie closer to me. "Nat, sea turtles lay their eggs together on beaches. When we have babies let's have them together."

"Sure, but not on the beach." She batted her eyelashes, and her black marble eyes laughed at me.

That was my first visit to Saint Catherine's. I'd never been in a church before. I didn't know what to expect. We pushed on the massive wood doors. Natalie stopped, dipped the three middle fingers of her slender right hand into a bowl.

"What's that?"

"Holy water. Do like me, cross yourself with it."

"It's cold," I said surprised and followed her moves.

The church was dark, lit only by the flames of votive candles reaching out of small red glass holders, and shafts of dim light coming through stained glass windows.

"This is neat," I whispered and breathed in the smell of melting wax.

We knelt before the altar. "In the name of the Father, the Son and the Holy Ghost." Natalie kissed the little gold cross she wore around her neck, and I kissed the small silver and blue Jewish star my grandparents had given me for Chanukah. For a split second I thought about kissing the metal dog tag that hung just below my Star of David. I fiddled with it, running the fingers of my right hand over the raised letters of my name.

We were the children of Red Paranoia in a Cold War that could heat up and thaw as easily as a defrosting steak, made to wear dog tags on chains around our necks to identify our maimed, mutilated, mangled, bombed, blown-up bodies. We were in an arms race with the Communists and always hanging in the air was the threat of nuclear weather.

Last year we set off our first H-bomb.

Two years ago Mrs. Campbell, my plump, red-haired, red-faced, third grade teacher who looked like a tomato, told us over and over in a voice that sounded like she had a clothespin on her nose, "These safety procedures might save your lives if we're bombed, so don't be afraid boys and girls. Say your first and last name and the letters Y-G-T-T. TJohn Wilkinson, Y-G-T-T. Natalie Palermo, Y-G-T-T. Darci Beriman, Y-G-T-T... You'll-Get-Through-This."

We cowered under our desks, huddled in our fears. And we were always instructed to face away from the risky classroom windows during the dismal air raid drills that stained our childhood calendar.

"Nat, it feels safe here. I don't think anything bad'll happen to us. The windows are great."

"Dar, that's Jesus up there," she said, pointing to the man of many colors set in fragments of stained glass and bathed in the waning light coming through the tinted window panel behind the altar.

"He looks sad. Do you have to marry him one day?"

"No silly, why do you ask?"

"Remember when you wore that white dress and veil, you looked just like a little bride practicing for a wedding."

"That was my first Holy Communion, when I got this gold

cross." She lifted the gold chain to her lips and ran the little man on the crucifix over her smile.

"Is that when you drank the pretend blood?"

"Yeah, but I'm not married."

"Who's that?" I asked nearing the stone woman.

Without so much as a breath in between, Natalie said, "Saint Catherine of Sienna she had twenty-four brothers and sisters when she was a girl Jesus appeared to her once he came with his blessed mother he put a ring on Catherine's finger and she was his bride."

It was April but I could feel winter under my turtleneck shirt as a chill that had nothing to do with the weather ran up my spine; when it reached the nape of my neck my head pirouetted in a tight, quick counterclockwise stir.

"Nat, I think Jesus is gonna visit me someday," I blurted out in an awed whisper.

"Dar, we'll both see Jesus one day," she assured me, "when we're in heaven."

Two nuns sweeping the floor with their long black habits approached us while we admired the white marble statue. The taller nun with the thick glasses said, "Hello Natalie. You know, girls, Saint Catherine always kept Jesus in her heart."

"Thank-you, Sister Mary Catherine," Natalie said as she elbowed me to leave.

Outside, the sky was low and dark gray like a wooly blanket under which Brooklyn would sleep that night. We ran the seven blocks home. When I reached Liberty Avenue I could see my father. He was wearing his brown suit. His rough construction worker hands were clasped tightly behind his back. He was pacing a small patch of sidewalk, to and fro, like a pendulum. My father stared at me, with his teeth clenched, and raised his thick hand. I flinched because I thought he was going to hit me. Instead he pointed in the direction of our second floor apartment. I knew as surely as if he had spoken that I was to go upstairs immediately.

My mother was waiting in the doorway, wearing her size-twelve beige, knit ribbed skirt and matching top with sheer, clingy stockings and beige heels. It was one of only two dress outfits she owned. She usually wore cotton housedresses. Under her knit skirt she was wearing a girdle with garters to hold up her seamed stockings. The girdle was like a tube, open at the waist and the bottom. She didn't wear underpants and a girdle at the same time. I envisioned her fine strawberry blond pubic hair coming from the bottom of the girdle like a fancy lace fringe. I'd seen my mother getting dressed many times.

My mother had a sour look on her face. "I told you to be home before it got dark," she said angrily. "Now we're late for Papa's." She abruptly raised my arms above my head, tugged the white turtleneck top off, pulled me into our musty windowless bathroom and quickly scrubbed my face and hands with a washcloth that was stiff from being sun dried on a clothesline in the alley. It left my face red and stinging. She put a clean white cotton blouse on me and tucked it into the green, pleated skirt I was wearing. Then my mother sat down on the closed toilet seat and yanked the rubber band from my hair. I stifled a yelp and winced in discomfort. She clumsily redid my ponytail with her stiff knobby knuckled fingers, pressed the brush hard against my forehead to unglue my sweaty bangs and rushed me down the narrow stairwell.

My father was in the driver's seat of his new two-tone blue Chevrolet Bellaire. It wasn't exactly new—five years old. But it was his new car and he had wanted his family to see it while it was still light outside. Obviously that wasn't going to happen. My mother sat up front with my father and I climbed into the back seat. My father's silent green eyes met mine in the rearview mirror. No one spoke; the only noise was the windshield wipers *whacking* away the rain during the five-minute drive to Milford Street.

Five

My father's two long-nosed, olive-complexioned brothers, their wives, his pasty-skinned sister, her nervous twitching husband and my seven cousins were all seated at the Passover table, which under the starched white cloths were actually Papa's sawhorses with wide planks of wood on top.

Grandma's eyes narrowed. She looked directly at my mother. "We're all waiting for you, it's the first *seder* night and you hold Papa up. What's the matter with you?"

My mother's long swan-neck began to turn red and blotchy. She bit her lower lip; her hazel eyes looked to the floor. "I'm sorry Riva, it's just that Darci—"

"Oh, don't give me any baloney about Darci," my grandmother said as she heaved her great round bosom and pushed the air with her hands.

"But, Grandma, it's my fault we're late… because I went to *church* with Natalie."

The table, set with ceremonial dishes and silverware used only at Passover, stretched throughout the small dining room and down the middle of the parlor. Everyone sitting in the two cramped rooms turned and looked at me in disbelief, as if I were an Egyptian pharaoh come to Passover *seder.*

My grandmother's nostrils opened wide. "Thank God, Papa doesn't understand English," she said. Then she turned her right hand sideways—put it into her mouth and bit down, all the while glowering at my mother.

My mother's face turned red as if she too had been washed with a rough cloth.

Mrs. Campbell's mantra swirled in my head like a protective potion… Darci Beriman, Y–G–T–T…Sela Beriman, Y–G–T–T …You'll–Get–Through–This.

My mother's charge was to raise me, and by Beriman standards she was doing a lousy job. I felt sorry for my mother. She was a good person, but at every turn she seemed thwarted by circumstance and convention. After that Passover *seder,* I began to notice there was always a bottle of Robitussin cough medicine on our kitchen countertop. When one was depleted, another appeared. Bottle after bottle, yet I never heard my mother cough.

"I'm not pinning ribbons on myself, but I came from the Bronx and I managed to get here on time," Anna, my father's older sister, said sarcastically.

"Enough already," Uncle Joe responded, pushing his right

hand, palm forward, gesturing for her to back off.

And so began the long Passover *seder*. At the head of the table, reclining on a wicker sun porch chair with two faded floral pillows, Papa read in Hebrew from a special prayer book, the *Haggadah*, and my uncles explained.

Uncle Joe said, "Papa's reclining as a sign of ease and the free status of the Israelites."

Uncle Sy, two years younger than my father and a year older than Joe, said, "We're celebrating the liberation of our ancestors."

Uncle Ben, Aunt Anna's nervous twitching husband said, "God in his love and mercy led them out of their suffering."

I wondered why he let them suffer to begin with.

Anna and Ben's daughter, my perky cheerleader cousin May, seated next to me, said, "See my new skirt, it has pictures of Queen Elizabeth."

"Yeah, I like it, it's neat."

"She's Queen of England. She's gonna have a coronation in…"

I interrupted her, "I know, in June."

May's blue eyes opened wide. "You're pretty smart, Dar. The coronation is June second."

Papa was saying benedictions and pouring blood red wine pressed from the grapes that grew on the side of his house.

Grandma was shuffling food platters.

Uncle Joe's little boy, Philip said he had to go to the toilet. His mother, Aunt Sid said, "So go, quickly."

The uncles were still explaining.

Uncle Joe said, "When the slaves fled Egypt they didn't have time for their bread to rise."

Papa lifted the white embroidered matzoh cover to reveal three pieces of unleavened bread. He broke the center matzoh. Pious and bent, he rose from the table and hid the matzoh somewhere in the house.

Uncle Sy said, "That's the *aphikoman*, it means dessert in Greek."

Uncle Ben, his eyes involuntarily blinking, said, "Whoever finds the *aphikoman* gets a quarter."

Later my cousins all went down to the basement in search of the twenty-five cent matzoh. Not me. Papa's basement was where my father's secret lived and I no longer considered it a holy place.

Papa set out a special glass of wine. My father loosened his tie and said in his booming voice, "That's for the prophet Elijah."

In syncopated rhythm to his twitching and blinking, Uncle Ben said, "The horseradish (twitch) is to recall (blink) the bitter life (twitch) of Israel during (blink) Egyptian bondage." (twitch)

I don't want to eat the horseradish that recalls the bitter life of Israel any more than I want to drink the blood and eat the body of Jesus. My family names the sacred Jewish. Natalie names the sacred Catholic. I want to be touched by the sacred. I want the winds of heaven to blow on me. I don't want to practice rituals and I don't want to wait until I die to see Natalie's Jesus in heaven.

My mother said, "Darci, no more wine for you."

"Her eyes are glazed over like donuts," my father said. "She looks like a grown-up with important things on her mind."

Six

I was in sixth grade. Grandma Riva was sick... she died. Six months later my grandfather died. My family mourned and mourned again.

My father said, "Papa died of a broken heart. He couldn't live without Mama."

"They were married forty-nine years," Uncle Joe said.

"Jeez, the years are moving. I'm thirty-six," my father boomed.

"Hey, I'm forty-six already," Aunt Anna chimed in, marking time like a clock.

⚜

It was late April, one month since Papa died. I woke up to a sparrow's warbling celebration of life. Across the alley, in the distance, the huge sycamore tree was filled with spring and there was no frost on the windowsill. I brush my teeth, and pee. I take off my pajamas and yesterday's underpants. I put on fresh white cotton panties, my white training bra and the rust color cardigan Natalie gave me for Christmas. I put the sweater on backwards with the small shiny buttons down my back and I tie a yellow bandana around my neck. I step into dungarees with wide rolled up cuffs, thick white bobby socks, a pair of dirty Keds the color of old snow and I tiptoe past my sleeping parents on the pull out sofa bed.

The spring air was minty and promising. I bounded around the corner to Natalie's, went directly to her ground floor bedroom window, *tapped-tapped-tapped* as I'd done a thousand times before. She didn't stick her smiling round moon face under the wood venetian blinds.

I called, "Natalie... Nat."

No answer. I went around to the front door and leaned against it so I could listen. The door cracked open just enough for me to see in. The living room was bare. The dilapidated couch and chair were gone. I walked in and stole past Mr. and Mrs. Palermo's bedroom into Natalie and Anthony's room. *Everything was gone*, their beds, Natalie's desk, Anthony's red toy chest. They must be in their parent's room. I pushed on the door slowly so I didn't wake them. With the door partially open I could see clearly that there was nothing in the room, no furniture, no Mr. and Mrs. P, no Anthony and no Natalie.

My Keds had wings. I flew around the corner and up the stairs.

I burst into the living room. My parents were still sleeping on the Castro convertible. I was trembling and crying.

My father bolted upright, "What's wrong?"

"Dad, no one's at Natalie's. They're gone. The furniture's gone. Everything is gone." My words were clipped with urgency.

My mother turned over like a flapjack and sat up with a scared look. "What's the matter?"

"Darci says the Palermo's apartment is empty and they're gone."

My mother said, "Calm down, Darci. Pini, go over there with her. I'm sure everything is fine."

I know by now that everything is far from fine. Still I'm hoping my father's eyes will see the worn blue camel back couch and the blue club chair right where they've been for the last four years and that my eyes have deceived me.

Dad put on a pair of gray work pants over his pajama bottoms. He left his tan pajama top on. Without socks he slipped into loafers and we walked back to Natalie's together.

The door was ajar. Dad walked in and looked around. I was behind him.

"Not a trace," he murmured. Then he said, "I'm sure everything is okay, Darci. Let's check with the manager."

We walked down Essex Street to the manager's unit. All the doors had the same semi-gloss bright green paint and tarnished knockers. My father lifted and lowered the doorknocker three times. Mrs. Martinico stuck her head outside and left her body inside behind the green door.

"Mr. Beriman, what's the problem?"

"Darci's friend Natalie, the Palermos, everything's gone from their place."

Mrs. Martinico stepped out from behind the door in a ratty white chenille bathrobe. She looked like she was wearing my bedspread.

"Waddaya mean everything's gone, their rent's paid for April."

My father pursed his lips and shook his head. I could see that his dark hair was beginning to recede.

"You mean you don't know anything about this?"

"No. Musta left in the middle of the night. Nice family. Sorry."

"Thanks for your trouble, Mrs. Martinico. Come on, Darci."

As soon as dad opened the green door to our hallway we could smell the coffee. Upstairs in our half-furnished cabbage patch my mother was making French toast. She dipped challah from Sugarman's Bakery into the beaten eggs and milk. She coated the bread, pulled it out of the red and white bowl and plopped it into the heavy iron skillet. It *sizzled* when it hit the hot butter. She flipped the toast over revealing a light brown crust and asked, "So?"

"So nothing," my father answered. "They're gone, lock, stock and barrel. Mrs. Martinico said they paid for the month."

"What about the bar where he works?" my mother inquired.

"You're a regular genius, Sela, like I know the name."

My father gets hot under the collar and my mother's neck gets predictably red and blotchy.

"Do you know the name?" she asked me softly.

I didn't know the name. Natalie was gone. My best friend.

She knew all my secrets, and I hers. We were going to live next door to each other. We were going to have our babies together. I drew a breath deep into my body. "Darci Beriman, Y-G-T-T...You'll-Get-Through-This."

We took turns at the table because we only had room for two chairs in the narrow kitchen. I ate my French toast with a glass of milk. My father had a cup of black coffee and waited for his piece. When I finished, my mother sat down and had her breakfast.

My stomach was in knots. I ran to the bathroom, got down on my knees in front of the toilet and threw up.

My mother felt my forehead with her soft lips. "Darci, you're warm. Stay in today honey. I'll make you some tea, you can rest in bed."

I didn't argue. I was tired, my stomach ached, my eyes were swollen with sadness and I wanted my friend Natalie. I sipped hot tea, and cried. I napped fitfully and dreamed about baby turtle eggs on exotic white sand beaches with palm trees that looked like grass skirted hula ladies, their rhythmic hips, milk-filled coconuts swaying in the breeze...and Natalie.

By nightfall I wasn't sleepy. My parents turned in for the evening and I lay awake in my closet-size bedroom overlooking the alley. Through the slats of the sagging venetian blinds, that like the green doors came with all the apartments, I could see the man in the moon. Grandma Riva once told me the man was imprisoned there as a punishment for breaking the Sabbath. I wondered if I was being punished for not honoring the Jewish traditions of my family. But I knew there was no man. I'd read at the library that one of his eyes is called the Imbrium Basin in the Sea of Rains and is a mammoth crater, maybe seven hundred miles wide.

I shut my own eyes tight to dispel any thoughts of punishment, and he was with me. Not the man in the moon, the man from the stained glass windows at Saint Catherine's. My mother was wrong. *Jesus is not a figment.* I automatically heard Mrs. Campbell's Y–G–T–T, but I was unafraid and I didn't use the mantra. He was beautiful and somehow sad looking. His hands bore the marks of the crucifixion. He stood in silence surrounded by a golden mist. I was filled with his glory. Then he was gone.

My stomach was cramping. I pulled the elastic waistband of my pajamas and my underpants away from my body with my left hand, and slipped my right hand down low to rub the sharp pain. My hand felt sticky. I removed it. It was red, bloody, I was having my first period. I remembered the first time I went to church with Natalie. The massive wood doors, the smell of melted wax. We dipped into the holy water bowl and crossed ourselves. I dip into the bowl between my legs, and with blood I make the sign of the cross on the inside of my hands. I lay with my hands at my sides and I wonder if Natalie has her period too, if she paints bloody crosses on her hands, if she sees Jesus before she goes to heaven. I sleep in an envelope of peace. In the morning I arise before the sun and before my parents. Using two safety pins I fasten a disposable pad to the sanitary belt my mother has lying in wait for me. I wash away the crosses, and scrub my blue flannel pajama bottoms and my cotton underpants. Natalie leaves an indelible mark that cannot be washed away as easily.

Seven

Uncle Sy, Uncle Joe, Aunt Anna and my father sold Papa's little red frame house with the bay window on Milford Street. My parent's share of the profit opened the door of the cramped tenement flat, finally releasing them.

"Darci, we're moving. You'll have a bigger room. Aunt Anna says she'll make a pink dust ruffle and coverlet for your bed, and new café curtains—pink. Dad and I'll have our own bedroom. We'll definitely get a television. There's a laundry room with a dryer; you'll make new friends," my mother rambled on with an excitement that could almost be mistaken for happiness.

꙳

I didn't get to vote on it and my family moved to Queens.

Along with the pink bedroom accessories, Aunt Anna brought me a bag of clothing that my cousin May had outgrown. In the bag I found the white full skirt with the pictures of Queen Elizabeth's coronation. I was wearing the skirt when I entered the elevator and met three other teenage girls who lived in my new building.

"Hi, I'm Darci."

As if on cue, the three girls raised their six eyes. Then they looked down at my skirt.

"I'm Rhona, this is Marlene, that's Fran."

The elevator stopped, the door opened and the four of us got out on the ground floor.

"Your skirt is kinda short," Rhona who was short herself, thick waisted and bespectacled said.

I cocked my head apologetically, "That's the style in London where I got the skirt."

"You've been to London?" Marlene the slim, red-haired, freckle faced potential beauty asked.

Before I could answer, Rhona chanted, *"Sure...you've been to London, Darci, Darci where have you been? I've been to London to visit the Queen. And what did you do there? I sat under her chair."*

The girls all laughed.

"Yeah, Darci sat under the Queen's chair," Fran the pinched face girl taunted.

"Well, I didn't sit under her chair but I did see the coronation," I told the mean-spirited girls as we moved outside the vestibule and stood in front of the imposing seven-story red brick building we all called home.

Marlene brushed a wisp of red hair away from her freckle dotted forehead and asked, "If you really were there, what's this?" She was pointing to the Queen's left hand.

I answered my jury of peers, "It's a rod with a dove. It symbolizes the Holy Ghost." I smoothed out a fold in my full skirt to show the picture more clearly. "See in her right hand she's holding a scepter. Look on top of it... that's the Star of Africa. It's the largest cut diamond in the world."

Rhona sniffed, "I don't believe you've been to London." But she didn't look so sure.

The following week Rhona Frank, Marlene Katz and Fran Goldberg were all wearing skirts that were unfashionably short. Still, the girls didn't give me entrance into their exclusive club of three and largely ignored me. I endured the unfriendly girls and made other friends.

I was unable to go to summer camp because "We don't have money for camp," my mother said.

I was unable to play an instrument because "We can't afford a piano, Darci."

"What about a violin, Mom?"

"Even if you got a used violin we can't afford the lessons."

My father was in and out of work, my mother drank cough medicine, and my training bra gave way to a C cup, Grandma Riva's legacy to me. I liked the way I looked; I especially liked the way boys looked at me.

٭

I was in tenth grade. My mother's excitement over the new apartment long since gone, she took on the sour-look as a permanent expression. I massaged my mother's swollen size-six feet and rubbed her aching legs every day when I returned from my after-school job at Lambston's Five and Dime.

My mother fell on the icy sidewalk. The shopkeepers came out to help her, but no one could help with the cancer. It ravaged her bones and when she died, two weeks before I graduated from Jamaica High, her long beautiful neck was gone. Her head was practically sitting on her shoulders.

Zion Funeral Home on Queens Boulevard was filled with family, friends, and neighbors from the building. Even the unfriendly girls paid their respects. I wished it were one of their mothers and not mine who was wrapped in the white burial shroud and laid out in a plain pine box.

I wanted to nestle my face next to my mother's. I wanted to kiss her goodbye. My father shook his head for me not to and he closed the flat pine top on the coffin. There was a little girl inside of me. Her face was pressed against the window of my loss. She was pleading, sobbing, wailing. I sat in quiet sorrow in the borrowed black dress, in the hard chair, in the unforgiving funeral home.

Rabbi Nexer was cutting the black mourner's ribbon pinned to my black dress. He slipped and the razor cut through the dress and into my flesh, right at my heart. Blood was gushing out. It hurt as much as if I had impaled myself on a sharp stake. I placed my hands over my heart to stop the bleeding. I looked down, but there was no blood. Only the ribbon had been cut. I could barely breathe. *I was sure that I was cut.* For a moment reality faded and only my memories were real. I'm with my mother at one of her chemotherapy sessions. We eat lunch in the clean hospital cafeteria. My mother takes a bite of her tuna on rye sandwich and it secretes a reddish fluid onto her lips and chin.

"Mom, wait here. I'll get you another sandwich."

Behind the counter the stocky man with short arms has sliced his pointer finger with a knife and blood is leaking out the sides of the band-aid wrapped around his swollen finger. The cafeteria lady working alongside the bleeding man quickly prepares another tuna fish sandwich. I return to the table but I do not tell my mother that the first tuna fish sandwich squirted her face with blood. My mother always says the chemo sessions leave her feeling like a slaughtered chicken without a head. I'm not going to add to my mother's queasiness.

The agonizing pain from the laceration in my heart of hearts was with me all day into the dark night. When I finally fell asleep in my pink bedroom, my dreams were filled with pink-breasted mourning doves, their gentle voices cooing sadly. I dreamt of Indian widows, draped in silk saris, throwing themselves on their dead husband's funeral pyres; of my mother's friend Pat McGuckin who threw herself on her husband Robert's grave and four months later married another man. I dreamt of the Egyptian pharaoh-god Osiris, who was murdered by the jealous god Set, his body cut into pieces and put into a box. His Queen, the goddess Isis, found his remains floating on the Nile. She put his body back together and Osiris was alive again.

My mother has not cheated death like Osiris, and my father and I sit *shiva*, the Jewish period of mourning, on low hard backless stools. For five days we receive visitors, food and condolences. I'm pleasant, even congenial, but I can't be here anymore. I simply can't. My aunts, uncles, high school friends—I need to be someplace else. I don't belong here. I'm going to explode, evaporate, tumble into an underground world like Alice, drink cough medicine like my mother.

Eight

I graduated from high school without fanfare. My aunts and uncles acknowledged my accomplishment with cash. And with the forty-seven dollars I'd saved from my dollar an hour job at the Five and Dime, I had one hundred and seven dollars. I was feeling stuck, planted like an old deep-rooted maple tree on Milford Street.

A week after graduation my father and I were eating breakfast together. It seemed so odd, we had room for three chairs at our table, but the one with my mother's imprint was empty. Dad reached across the pink faux marble formica top of the wrought iron table and placed a worn manila envelope in my hand.

"Darci, mother wanted you to have a nice... a special wedding. She was saving money since you were little. This is from mother for you."

My breathing turned shallow even before I knew that envelope contained summer camp, music lessons, and an instrument never to be played. I managed a closed lip smile and peered inside to a boodle of money. I couldn't believe my eyes. There were hundred dollar bills, which in my mind represented a hundred ways my mother deprived herself. I excused myself to the bathroom; stood with my back against the door and counted the money. Three, four, six... seven one hundred dollar bills. This is unbelievable and clearly my way out of the past into the future. I loved my father and I was concerned about him. But I knew his sister and brothers would look after him. Besides, I was being guided to the edge of a different experience. Sorry, Mom, but I'm not using this money for a wedding. I'm using it for a divorce, from Queens, from New York. Even my parent's look-a-likes Lucille Ball and Desi Arnaz, television's golden couple, are no longer married. *It appears that if life is about anything it's about change.*

I lay in bed that night like a flightless bird whose deficient wings would soon be full and perfect, imagining where I'd go. I didn't consider what I'd do when I got there.

⁂

My entire family had its feathers ruffled. The aunts and uncles were holding a powwow at our apartment in Queens. Aunt Anna, seated next to my father on the rose sofa, looked a lot like papa, with pasty pale gray skin. Her brown hair was almost all silver and a few gray chin whiskers stood out stiffly. She was about my height, five-six.

Her blue veined legs were dangling and her tapping feet called attention to the twined rose fringe edging the bottom of the sofa. It had been my grandparent's sofa and had seen better days. The damn fringe wouldn't stay attached; it kept coming down. I'd sit on the floor and sew it up before we had company. I wasn't doing that anymore and part of the fringe was lying on the rose carpet.

"Your mother's not cold in the ground yet and you're leaving her," Aunt Anna stormed.

As if my staying could alter my mother's temperature.

"The Mediterranean—mama left to come here—you're going back to the Old World. Why, why would you do such a thing?" Uncle Sy asked incredulously.

"Greenwich Village is so cool. Why would you leave New York?" my cousin May asked, pop-eyed.

"I have to leave here. I have to find out who I am."

"You don't know who you are," my aunt said. "Ask me, I'll tell you who you are. Darci Beriman, that's who. Queens College is walking distance from this apartment and you're going to the Mediterranean. Flowers bloom where they're planted."

I wonder whose life is more tainted, my cousin May's with her domineering insufferable mother or my new existence as a motherless daughter.

Aunt Anna gave me a look. The look seemed to carry with it some Beriman ancestral intervention into the affairs of the living. I didn't back down. I tried to explain that I was restless, that I was like a bird summoned to a far off spring, but I couldn't explain. Not even to myself.

Grandma Riva once told me that someday I should go to the basin. She called it that. "The basin is a special place. You might discover the river beneath the river there."

I protested, "Grandma, the Mediterranean's a sea, not a river."

She elevated her rotund chest in her inimitable way, pointed her finger at me and said, "Child, this is true, but it's a sea that has one current on the surface and another that flows deep beneath, just like with people. Darcilah, you go, you'll learn many things."

"I learn a lot at the library, in school."

"There are schools in the basin, too." Then she added, almost imperceptibly, "Mystery schools."

Wagging his long narrow Beriman nose, Uncle Joe said, "It's a shame, a young girl goes off on her own."

"A foreign country to boot," his wife, Aunt Sid said.

And from Uncle Ben, Aunt Anna's nervous husband, a whining, "*Oy vey*, never a dull moment in this family."

My indignant relatives left, the smell of cigarette smoke lingered, and fear moved across my father's face like an eclipse.

"I'm worried about you goin' so far away on your own."

"I'll be fine, Dad. I'll send postcards from all over." I stroked his thick arm. "I love you."

"I love you too, Darci," he said uneasily as he got up and walked out of the rose colored living room.

Part Two

Nine

I climbed up the steel ramp. A warm breeze caught the bib of
my sailor blouse and lifted it up around my shoulders like flapping wings. A bird flies away leaving it's nest behind. I wasn't
connected enough to feel as if I were leaving my home behind. I
still identified with turtles, hatched out of eggs, never knowing
their parents and carrying their shelter with them. But for the
first time it really occurred to me that birds too are born out of
eggs. My heart was pumping excitedly, my stomach a quivering
slab of nervous energy, and my own wings took form when I
boarded the Boeing 707 at Idlewild, headed for Greece. No more
ponytail; my dark brown hair was in a short stylish pixie. The
knee length black and white check gingham straight skirt, the
white sailor-blouse with matching black and white tie and the
black patent leather pumps were new, not hand-me-downs. The

two seats next to mine were already occupied. I stowed my black leather shoulder bag under the aisle seat.

"Hi, I'm Darci Beriman."

"Darci love, it's a pleasure," said the gorgeous raven-haired woman seated next to me. "This is my husband, Michael Drummond." She turned to the good-looking man, then back to me. "I'm Olivia Drummond."

Michael gave me a de luxe welcoming smile, locked eyes with mine and said, "We're delighted to meet you."

His smile was slightly crooked. It made him look rugged. They both looked twenty-two, -three or -four. Olivia's glossy black straight hair was parted in the middle and reached her shoulders. She was wearing black Cleopatra eyeliner that accentuated her black eyes, and on her full lips baby pink lipstick, the color of her silk suit. There was a little space between her upper two front teeth, and her teeth were the whitest I'd ever seen. Her husband had light brown hair and deep blue almost indigo eyes.

"Are you New Yorkers?" I asked.

"I grew up in Los Angeles," Michael answered.

"Oh, that's why your hair is so cool looking."

He chuckled, "Actually we were in England, saw these musicians …McCartney, Lennon, Harrison and this other guy, Browne. The Quarreymen. Talk about cool. Their hair was like this."

"I love their hair and convinced Michael it's his style," Olivia added in an elegant accent.

"Where are you from, Olivia?"

"Crete."

"Crete! That's where my grandmother was from."

"It is special place." She touched her heart.

I couldn't help noticing the huge solitaire diamond ring she wore. It made my mother's engagement diamond look like a speck, not that I'd seen my mother's ring all that often. It was in hock at the pawnbroker's shop more then it was on her finger.

"My parents have olive orchards on Crete and Michael exports olive oil." She raised her dark eyes. "The rest is history."

"Olivia of the olive orchards and the olive husband—that makes you the olive queen."

Olivia pressed her baby pink lips together. Michael readjusted himself in his window seat. My mouth went dry embarrassed by its own voice.

"Sorry, I've gotten off on the wrong foot with you guys. I didn't mean to hurt your feelings."

"Darci love, don't be upset," she said. "Please, is nothing, is okay. We try to stay away from sour jokes. Remember our mouths are attached to our brains, hopefully also to our hearts. Believe me, we are not always successful."

I began reading *The Fountainhead*; Olivia was reading too. Michael pointed out the familiar New York City skyline. I leaned forward and craned to see through the small window. How peculiar, now that I'm leaving New York, from this perspective it looks fascinating.

"One of a kind, you can always recognize it," he said.

"Yeah, but I'm happy to be leaving. I've wanted to get away from here forever."

"You might consider being happy about going toward Greece and not away from New York."

I closed my eyes for a moment. "That's interesting, Michael. I've never thought of it that way, happy about goin' toward something and not away from something. Yeah, I like that."

"You're quick," he said, covering a yawn with his hand.

We read, we napped, we shared snacks, we talked. We talked a lot. Michael was asleep now. Olivia and I chatted on.

"What are your plans when you get to Greece?" she asked.

"I wanna visit the Acropolis, stand in that history; visit the old city."

"Ah, the Plaka, this is a must, so lively."

"And of course Crete where my grandmother was. . ."

"Do you speak any Greek?"

"Only a few words. My grandmother spoke several languages, but she favored Spanish. . . taught it to me. Her family was Jewish, expelled from Spain. Scattered to Morocco, Turkey, ended up on Crete."

Olivia lowered her black Cleopatra-lined eyelids. "Another sad chapter in history, all in name of religion. Well, at least you can follow Jewish or whatever you want in America."

"I'm still searching for something that feels right. I'm not practicing Judaism. What about you?"

"I was raised in Greek Orthodox, and Michael in Catholic Church. We enjoy the traditions, also we honor spirit in our own way."

I wondered what she meant by honoring spirit in her own way

but I didn't want to be rude and pry beyond the information she had offered.

I awoke from a nap. Olivia offered me a piece of chocolate. "Thanks, I love chocolate." I bit down on the small dark mound and sighed at the sweet sensation on my tongue. "Please have some raisins." I handed the bag to Olivia. She took some, then passed the bag on to Michael who was awake now.

"Love, we are stay in Athens for two days; then we go on to Crete. Why don't you join us? We stay with my parents. They have plenty of room and they adore visitors."

"Are you sure?"

"Yes, of course!" she said, then turned to her husband, "Michael, you..."

"Join us, you'll have fun," he answered before she could finish.

I folded my hands in my lap and sat very still. Here I was flying all by myself, with limited money, to a strange country. This couple was a godsend. I felt so comfortable with them, like I'd known them forever. I knew I could trust them. I thought about my family's concern and how my life was like a jigsaw puzzle that somehow would all fit together, but I certainly didn't know that one of the pieces would be the Drummond's.

"Darci love, in Athens my parents keep a suite at Grande Bretagne. You can stay with us, has two bedrooms, two baths. We can show you around the Plaka, after you visit Acropolis."

"I'd love to stay with you."

"Yes, then you must. We'll be on Crete for one month before we return home."

"Oh, I thought you lived on Crete."

"No, my parents are there. Michael has business to take care of and this way I go see my family. We were in America because, sadly, Michael's father died. We go to help his mother. So now we visit my family, then back to Barcelona."

"I'm sorry to hear about your father, Michael."

"Thanks...it's not easy...but only people die, the loving remains."

"Yeah, the loving does remain. How's your mother?" I asked.

"It's been tough on her. They were high school sweethearts."

Suddenly the plane jolted. Startled, I jumped. It felt as if the plane was falling out under me.

"That's the wheels coming down. We'll be landing soon." Michael spoke with the ease of someone comfortable flying.

"Darci, why don't you change seats with me so you can see."

"*Efaristo*, Michael."

"*Parakalo*. You're welcome."

The plane descends into Athens. I see at once the luminous break of day and a pale crescent moon on the horizon. The blue Mediterranean sky oozes into infinity. It takes my breath away.

Ten

Lately everything takes my breath away. The afternoon sun places its hand upon Crete, fingerpaints it with a dazzling white-blue light. The Acropolis rises above Athens, its Doric columned Parthenon, temple to Athena, stands tall amongst her people who bow perpetually to the goddess. The marble bath at the Grande Bretagne. Only a week ago I was in my parent's, my father's small bathroom with its cracked pink floor tiles.

"It is Kazantzakis."

"That's a hard one."

"No, it is easy, Darci. Listen... Ka-zan-tsah-kis."

"Easy for you, Olivia," I laughed. "Okay, I got it —Nikos Ka-zan-tsah-kis."

"That is it, love, perfect. He was one of our great writers, born here on Crete. He wrote *Zorba the Greek*."

"I've heard of that book. I see he died three years ago."

We were standing under a cross tall as a telephone pole, at his lone gravesite by the side of a road near a bluff overlooking the Mediterranean.

"Look at the mountains over there, what do you see?" Michael asked.

I turned and looked. "A man's head."

Michael smiled. "They say that's the head of Zeus. You can only see it from this place on the island."

"Amazing… what does this say?"

Olivia translated the inscription on the simple gray memorial stone, *"I am afraid of nothing, I want nothing, I am free."*

The epitaph roared through my mind, reverberating as though it were in an echo chamber. I could feel his liberation, his exemption from fear. A chill went up my spine. When it reached the nape of my neck my head jerked quickly in a tight counter-clockwise stir. I was having an epiphany of sorts.

"Someday," I said, "I'm gonna live those words: I am afraid of nothing, I want nothing, I am free."

Michael smiled, he smiled a lot, and as always his mouth was a tad off kilter. "I'm sure you will. Ere Zeta says spirit meets us at the point of our action. Your being here, it's a step on your journey toward freedom, enlightenment. Of course, he says we're already enlightened, we just don't know it."

"Is Ere Zeta a Spanish author?" I asked.

"He's a teacher and he writes books."

"What does he teach?"

"About spirit, about the soul. Some say it as the teachings of the mystery schools."

I stood frozen for several long seconds, then I took a step forward and repeated Michael's words. "The mystery schools. My grandmother once spoke of them. Of all the people in the world I could sit next to, how'd I get so lucky to sit next to you two?"

"They say coincidence is God working and preferring to remain anonymous."

"I like that, Michael. God remaining anonymous. So there is no coincidence."

"Perhaps when you visit us in Spain you'll meet Ere Zeta."

"Is that an invitation, Olivia? Because if it is, the answer is yes —Yes! I love you guys."

Olivia's smile was huge. I could see the little gap between her teeth as she said, "Ah, the heart is opening. A sure sign you are ready."

Michael added, "And they say when the student is ready the teacher shall appear."

※

July 2,1960

Dear Dad,
The flight was long. No monsters rising out of the sea. I arrived safely. Olivia sat next to me and has taken me under her wing. I stayed with her family for a few days. Now I'm at a guesthouse on Crete with students from different countries (they all speak English). I'm going to assist with an archeological dig (free room and board). Olivia got me placed on the project. I'm doing great. Hope all is well.

Love, Darci

P.S. photo is the Parthenon

Eleven

The old whitewashed guesthouse with its flaming purple bougainvillea-covered veranda and red barrel-tiled roof was pleasant and modest—no marble bath, just a shower room with metal hooks on the walls, a few long wood benches and three showerheads. The white paint was crackled, lifting in places, and a slight mildew odor mingled with a hint of bleach came from the drain.

The five young men waited to clean up until after my roommate and I showered. She was the only other female on the dig. Five-ten, blonde, smart, from Denmark. I liked her and the small tidy room with twin beds we shared on the first floor.

Our seriously bronze-skinned, curly-haired team leader held a meeting. "On this dig archaeologist will refer to us by our country or city's name. So call me Mykonos." He adjusted his sunglasses low down on his Herculean nose and told us he had good news, we were going to see first hand what archaeology had produced. "Comfortable boots and hats are must. Be ready in morning, half-past five. We meet here in dining room. Any questions?"

"Where are we going?"

"It is surprise, Boston. Tomorrow archaeologist will tell us."

⁂

We were noisy, fired up at breakfast, passing plates of feta, juicy tomato slices, dark olives, and the coffeepot which left a trail of steam in our midst.

Mykonos ripped his hot roll apart, dipped a piece in olive oil and asked, "How many archaeologist it takes to discover buried city?"

"Seven."

"Close, Denmark. Takes one archaeologist to find it, seven assistants to dig up."

While Mykonos chowed down on his roll, all the assistants groaned in unison and eyes flicked around the long family-style dining table acknowledging the riddle's clever answer as a mockery of the truth.

A stout man of medium height wearing khaki cotton pants, a long sleeve khaki shirt and worn laced boots with a safari hat in one hand and a cigarette in the other introduced himself in a raspy voice, "Young ladies and young gentlemen, good morning."

"Good morning, sir," we echoed back.

He told us his name was Doctor Joseph Evans, that archaeology ran in his family's blood. "At the turn of the century, my cousin Sir Arthur Evans started to excavate the palace at Knossos. Today we'll head off to Knossos on the north central coast."

Denmark and France had been flirting with each other all morning. They rushed onto the bus and sat in the last row together. I sat next to Africa on the bus. With wide set eyes that twinkled and short wooly hair, he was handsome, dark, smart and sensitive. We became fast friends.

"You think I'm tall?"

"I'd say six-four."

"One hundred eighty-three centimeters to feet, you're correct, America, six feet almost four inches. Some Nilotes stand seven feet and more."

"What's Nilote?" I asked.

"The tall, slender ones in Africa. My father is Nilote, my mother's people are Yoruba from Nigeria. Your family?"

"I'm taller than my mother. She was five-three." I held my hand sideways across the tip of my nose and thought how different our noses were. Mine long narrow and straight, his broad down the middle and flaring at the nostrils. "My father is my height."

"Ah, like the Yoruba. My grandfather is a Yoruba tribal king."

"That makes you a *prince*," I said somewhat astounded.

He lowered his twinkling eyes and asked about my father.

"He builds skyscrapers. He worked on the Empire State Building."

"I've been to New York City. Have you ever been to Africa?" he asked.

I laughed, "No, I was never on an airplane before I came here."

"Someday you must come to Tanganyika. You have heard of Mount Kilimanjaro?"

"Sure."

"It's in Tanganyika. Lake Victoria, Africa's largest. On the Serengetti Plain we have giraffes, tall like the Nilotes." A look of pride came into his eyes. "Elephants, zebras, lions, leopards—all in Tanganyika."

"It sounds incredible. I can't imagine what it's really like. Your English is great."

"English and Swahili are both official. I'm one of the lucky ones to have a good education, to be here."

"Me too, Africa."

"Now that you're all secure on the bus, we're on our way to the palace. I must tell you," Dr. Evans let out a belch of smoke that trailed alongside his raspy voice. "Legend has it King Minos kept a horrible creature in the labyrinth at Knossos."

Africa called out, "The Minotaur."

Dr. Evans grinned and nodded. "The Athenians say every year King Minos sacrificed seven young men and seven maidens to the monster with a bull's head and a man's body. We have exactly seven assistants. If we add you to the group we sacrificed last summer we'll meet our quota."

Laughter filled the bus.

France asked, "This monster is mythical, right, Dr. Evans?"

"Young man, all of Greece is mythical. When you come here, so too are you."

There was a moment of profound human stillness that contrasted sharply with the noise of the clacking rattling old school bus. The silence was shouting in my head, America you're walking with gods and goddesses. You're part of this great mythological landscape.

Dr. Evans continued that according to legend Minos was the son of Zeus and Europa. In my mind's eye I could see Zeus high above Crete, his majestic head carved into the mountain range.

We reached Knossos around seven AM and walked through the palace remains for hours. So many passageways, I'm transported back thousands of years into the legendary labyrinth. I'm only steps ahead of the Minotaur. I must escape; I have so much to live for, so much to discover. I must find out who I am. I call upon Zeus. The palace artists and skilled craftsmen stop work on their intricate mosaics, pottery, bronze jewelry and elaborate wall frescoes. They cheer and applaud loudly as Zeus steps down from the mountain and carries me to safety.

The sky spits out crackles of thunder and lighting bringing me crashing back to reality. Rain pelts the north end of the island. Our exploration of Knossos is complete and we're all psyched for our own dig tomorrow.

Twelve

"America, you're bright eyed, bushy tailed for five-thirty."

"I'm excited, Boston. Are we the first ones?"

The fat-cheeked, baby-faced prep school boy answered with another inane cliche, the one about the early bird getting the worm. As if that weren't bad enough I shot back I hoped they weren't serving worms for breakfast.

"No, but we're sure to see some on the dig," he replied.

"Yeah, I never thought of that."

"I can tell you're from New York, you say 'yeah' instead of 'yes'."

"Why, they don't say 'yeah' in Boston?"

"We speak the king's English in *Bahston*. We *pahk* our *cahs*, we go to *Havahd*."

I didn't like Boston. He had an attitude about my friendship with Africa. His judgmental glances when we sat next to each other on the bus cast a shadow darker than black skin could ever be. I wanted to tell him to shut up, but I didn't. I just said, "Yeah, I mean yes. My mother's friend Pat McGuckin came from Boston. She spoke like that."

"Good morning, Miss America."

"Good morning, Miss Denmark. You were snoring when I got up."

"I do not snore," she replied in a silly high-pitched voice.

"No you don't. I'm kidding, but you were sleeping."

"Hi, Denmark, hi, America, Boston."

"Good morning, France," we answered back, then we greeted Istanbul and Africa.

Even though it was still dark outside, Mykonos was wearing his sunglasses. He strutted into the low-ceilinged dining room, raised his arms and fists in the air and exclaimed, "You're all here before me, excellent kick ass team!"

⚜

The excavation is precise, dirty work. We're all careful not to unduly disturb the site. We're looking for pottery and potsherds. We dig with small picks, trowels, spoons, sieves and with our hands.

Dr. Evans says when we come across an artifact to stop immediately and call him. Two weeks into the dig he notices a depression in the ground and calls for a plaster of paris mix. None of the assistants know what's going on, but everything comes to a halt.

Dr. Evans pours the quick setting paste into the hole in the ground. We wait for it to harden. He digs around it with a knife. Sweat trickles down his fleshy brow. The assistants are silent. Even the archaeologists are stunned when Dr. Evans reveals the perfect cast of what he identified as a *bouzouki*. The long-necked stringed instrument resembling a mandolin long ago disintegrated leaving the empty space. Photographs and soil samples are taken. We usually dig in the mornings. Today we work right into the blazing afternoon heat.

By the time I returned to the three-story guesthouse I was khaki from head to toe, fatigued and the last to the shower. Precariously balancing my clean clothes, underwear, shampoo, soap, comb, washcloth and towel in my arms I backed into the room. I piled everything on the low bench and closed the door with my foot. Floating around somewhere between exhaustion and the Minotaur I was oblivious and didn't hear the water. I looked up. Africa was there, clear water caressing his darkness. His body was taut, muscular, his penis uncircumcised. He didn't turn away ashamed. He looked directly at me. His thick eyelashes were two cups holding droplets of water. His black eyes bright, encouraging as beacons in a storm inviting me in.

"The others don't shower with me," he said in a low, tired voice.

"I'll shower with you," I said boldly, despite the lump I was feeling in my throat.

I stepped under the running water with my clothes on. The lukewarm water swirling around the drain turned a muddy color. I ran my fingertips across his lathered chest. "I love this scent."

"The soap, it's made with African spices, clove oil," he answered.

I wanted that scent to permeate my body. To seep down through the familiarity that lived below my skin, deep into the aquifer of my stored memory.

Africa brought his long, thin fingers to my face. "America, you'll get in trouble. I must go."

I looked into his eyes. "Only if you meet me later down by the bay," I prompted.

He paused, then shook his head yes. In one long stride he moved out of the shower and left me to clean myself. I watched him. He's full in all the right places I mused, his rear, his lips, his penis. Of all the splendid flora and fauna to come out of Africa the black man was by far the most extraordinary.

⁂

After dinner everyone retired early. By nine the house was asleep. Barefoot and filled with longing, for what I had only fantasized about, I sneaked past Denmark. Outside the air was pregnant with the fragrance of lavender. It reminded me of my grand-mother. Damp sand stuck to the bottom of my feet as I made my way under wild fig trees down a winding path to the beach.

He was waiting with a half-amused smile on his noble face. Any fear I had of being discovered and dismissed from the dig was swept away by a feverish excitement surging through my body. I stepped out of my white cotton shorts and pulled my tee shirt off over my head. I unbuttoned his shirt. He took off his khaki shorts. Under a canopy of Mediterranean stars we bathed together. We splashed and swam and frolicked like a pair of young dolphins in a hidden grotto, a familiar spawning ground. I felt a shell wedged under my foot. Africa dove down and plucked the shell from between my toes. When he broke the surface of the water he was holding the tiny shell, no bigger than the nail of my pinky finger. He placed his hand over my flat belly. Spreading his long fingers like a black coral fan he tucked the shell into the fold of my belly button. He had brought along the bar of spiced soap and we washed each other. Slowly, deliberately my hands explored his body as if it was *Africa* itself.

"My people say the first man you're with is the father of your first born—even if the baby comes many years after. They say the baby is hiding, waiting to be born later from a *bisisi*, a long pregnancy. It's said you have a *bisisi* child. Are you sure you want me to…"

Of course I was sure. I had wanted to be with a dark-skinned man since I was a child, since my introduction to dirty words. Yes I wanted him to be my first lover, my first man. I wrapped my legs high around him. Buoyed by the water I lay back and floated weightless as sea foam. Long, salty kisses. His breath flowed over my lips like a whisper. He leaned forward and kissed my breasts, circling first one eager nipple with his tongue and then the other. I arched my back and sighed the sounds of pleasure. He ran his hand over the triangular mound of my dark silky hair and tenderly slipped his finger into the juicy passion below. I didn't say "fuck me" to this ebony prince. He placed his royalty inside of me and in the calm, phosphorescent sea we made love.

꙳

"America, there's a chill in the air," he said gently drying my body with his towel.

"Look, Africa, the North Star."

He lifted his gaze and asked me if I knew why the Little Bear's tail was stretched like that.

"No," I shook my head from side to side. "What little bear? That's the Little Dipper."

"Ah, it's also Ursa Minor." He told me that Zeus was in love with the nymph Callisto and to protect her from his jealous wife, Hera, who tried to kill her, he turned Callisto into a bear. "But Callisto's son, Arcas, didn't know the bear was his mother. He tried to kill it." Africa paused for a moment.

"Whoa," I interjected. "Greek mythology really gets under the covers with family stuff."

He broke into a brilliant smile that competed with his twinkling eyes and continued, "Then Zeus turned Arcas into a bear. To keep mother and son safe he pulled them both into the sky by their tails."

I pressed against his hard, damp, naked body. "The North Star will always remind me of you, Africa, and of this night, and Crete."

He dried my short wet hair and sent me back ahead of himself.

꙳

In the secrecy of night, under the cover of balmy salt air we meet and make love twice more. Our bodies rise and fall like the undulating sea. And in the bowl between my legs the exquisite pulsing, throbbing, drumming that is Africa stays with me through August, through the summer of my aliveness, the summer of my delight.

Thirteen

Sept. 5, 1960

Dear Dad,

The dig is over and the archaeologists have returned to their teaching positions. The experience was invaluable and some of the people I've met are even more precious than the treasures we unearthed. I'm with friends from Denmark and France on Mykonos. We're staying with our team leader's family (they make premium sausages that remind me of the ones at St. Catherine's Festival). Next week I leave for Spain to visit Olivia. Hope all is well.

Love, Darci

P. S. photo is Mykonos Harbor

⚜

"Darci love, thank you for sausages. Very thoughtful of you."

"You're welcome, Olivia."

"They make best sausages on Mykonos. Did you have fun there?" she asked.

"It was fantastic. We rode all over on scooters. I love the way the whole island… the houses are white, the sea's so blue. All those little churches… the windmills on the hill overlooking the boats in the harbor. Mykonos is enchanting."

"We have a gift for you, too," Michael said, smiling crookedly and handing me a book.

"*Zorba the Greek*. Thanks you guys. I'll treasure it."

"Actually we were hoping you'd read it."

"Michael, you are so bad," Olivia poked him playfully.

Michael and Olivia Drummond's house was spectacular. It had been an old bank, a narrow building with a gently sloping roof and three floors, which Michael renovated and Olivia decorated eclectically. The dining room used to be the vault. Now the dining room led into the kitchen, which led into a pantry and the maid's room. In the central hallway a curved staircase linked the lower and upper levels. The master suite was a complex in itself. The library-study had sky blue silk drapes and upholstery. The bathroom was sumptuous with a floor-to-ceiling mosaic mural of a nude mother and child. The mother giving breast to her infant. The sleeping area was unlike anything I had seen before. The bed was flanked on both sides by tall iron candelabra, and colorful hand-woven Moroccan carpets adorned the white travertine floor. Michael said that the king size bed's inlaid mother of pearl headboard had come from a Turkish harem.

"In that case," I said, "the bed ought to be called sultan-size."

Olivia and Michael exchanged smiles and they both fixed their eyes on me as we climbed the curved staircase to the third-floor guestroom. The room was romantic with a stone fireplace, and mahogany four-poster bed floating in layers of soft white cotton linens, a fluffy comforter and plush pillows, probably down. Back home our bedding was muslin, the scratchy kind with big cheesy flowers that do not resemble anything in nature.

I arose late the next morning. The house was abuzz with activity. Rosa, the housekeeper, was pounding squid. Michael was grinding coffee beans. An earthy aroma filled the long rectangular kitchen.

"Good morning sleeping beauty," Olivia flashed her pearly whites and greeted me.

"I felt like a princess in that bed."

"You slept well?" Michael asked.

"Like a log," I looked over at the gelatinous mounds of squid and shrieked, "*Dios*, they remind me of some of the boys I dated in high school with all those arms!"

Rosa, obviously embarrassed, clutched the over-sized silver cross on the chain around her neck and grimaced at my remark. The lines at the sides of her nose going down past her small mouth deepened and made her old, leathery face look like that of a marionette.

Olivia giggled like a schoolgirl and said, "Talk in English, love, and please have breakfast. Then I will teach you to make calamari. Also you can help me arrange flowers."

I sat down at the large rustic table in the center of the kitchen, had a cup of coffee, a poached egg and a piece of thick whole wheat bread spread with grape jelly. Olivia told me we were having company for dinner, Ere Zeta.

"Wonderful."

"Yes, is wonderful when he visits," she said moving to the table and reaching for one of the squid. "Okay, we cut arms into little rounds like this," she said wielding the knife expertly. "You mix flour, oil and egg yolks. Keep stirring and I add beer." She paused, thrusting the knife into the chopping block. "Good, now we put in ice box. Later we add beaten egg whites. Rosa will deep fry and we have calamari. Food for the gods."

Olivia and Michael's record collection was as eclectic as their home. Ray Charles' *Georgia On My Mind*, the Shirelle's *Dedicated To The One I Love* and Elvis' *Are You Lonesome Tonight* accompanied us as we prepared salad with lots of tomatoes, olives and chunks of feta. In between layering eggplant and ground beef for the moussaka, we stomped around the kitchen to fiery *Flamenco*. Setting the dining room table with starched white linen, fine china and sterling silverware, Olivia and I serenaded each other with our cockney and aristocratic interpretations of *My Fair Lady's* "The rain in Spain falls mainly on the plain." We filled hand-painted vases and crystal bowls with sunflowers round and full as smiling children's faces while Pachelbel's *Canon in D* played on the stereo and moved in my heart in some deeply visceral way.

With everything prepped and in place, we took a long siesta. When I came downstairs, rested, bathed and dressed in a long green skirt and green cap-sleeve blouse for dinner, Michael and Olivia were still in the master suite on the second floor. There was a warm golden glow emanating from the living room. I was surprised because it wasn't cold enough for a fire. When I entered fully into the step-down room, furnished with brown leather couches and chairs that had enormous rolled arms, I saw that the slate fireplace had not been lit.

"Hello, Darci," a voice that was at once soothing as an elixir and piercing as the truth greeted me, and I felt as though an electric current was coursing through my body.

"Ere Zeta?" I asked, stunned.

"Yes."

"But I, I know you. I... I've seen you... you were in my dream last night," I stammered.

"Yes," he said again.

"Really, I saw you. God, you probably think I'm crazy."

"No, Darci, I don't think you're crazy. That happens for some people. They dream of me before we meet," he said in perfect, unaccented English.

"At one time in my dream, Ere Zeta you wore a long hooded robe. When I looked closely you were a woman, but I knew it was you."

"The form I take is of no importance. The teachings of the

mystery school are not about who I am. The teachings exist to awaken you to who you are."

Moving toward the couch and taking a seat next to him I said, "I'd love to know who I am. I've never really felt comfortable with myself, since I was in first or second grade."

"There's a veil of forgetfulness placed with all infants; it descends by the time they are seven or eight."

"Why?"

"To keep the divine plan for your life and your past lives from being revealed."

"But why?"

"So you come to this life's experiences anew."

"You know, I feel different since I've met Olivia and Michael, more like I fit in."

"Because they're living in loving, caring and sharing; in health, wealth and happiness. Your soul recognizes that and wants that," he said.

"Yes, I, I think so. Can I come to the mystery school?"

"Yes, Darci, because you asked. It's a requisite for receiving the guidance of the masters." He looked directly into my eyes and said, "The spirit doesn't come to you until you come to it."

"Is the school here in Barcelona?"

Ere Zeta grinned impishly, "It's a school of inner travels, of an inner journey."

"You mean like in dreams?"

"Precisely, and when you learn to tune into the frequency of spirit, it's during your awake time as well."

"How do I tune in?"

"You start by loving yourself and you begin to remember you're a spiritual being on the way home to God."

"Do I have to die to go home to God?"

"You don't have to die to claim the grace of God. We're in a constant state of revelation and we can know the knowable, but not the unknowable. Your eyes are the same lovely green color as your skirt and blouse. What are you going to wear twelve years from today?"

"I have no idea."

"Because right now you don't need to know twelve years from now. It's part of the unknown."

Ere Zeta reached out and took my hand when Olivia and Michael joined us. Olivia, striking in a simple black sleeveless sheath, ushered us into the elegant dining room. Michael opened the high shuttered windows. We could smell the Mediterranean as if it had exhaled right into the house. In the glow of candlelight I looked at my friends and at Ere Zeta. They seemed somehow ethereal and angelic to me. I only had a little bit of sangría but felt as if I were lifting out of my body. Dinner was delicious. The conversation was lively and topical. Ere Zeta was a world traveler; he spoke about Light centers on the planet where he met with people of like mind who wanted to go into spirit while they were still here in the physical.

That night in the four-poster bed under layers of soft white cotton I slept like a princess again, and again I dreamt of Ere Zeta. Each time I saw him over the next two months he appeared differently. Was he young, old, thin, robust, curly or straight haired, fair skinned or did he have that genetic tan so common in Spain; how tall was he? Only his eyes were constant—but not in their color, rather in their quality of compassion, loving and wisdom. They were ancient, diaphanous eyes. Ere Zeta defied description. He was vibratory, dynamic, transubstantial both in my dreams and when I met with him while awake, during September and October.

On September twenty-fourth we strolled along the narrow cobblestone streets in the medieval quarter of Barcelona. The people were celebrating Our Lady of Mercy. Some donned huge ceremonial masks; others held elaborate *gigantes*, giant ten-foot puppets. Ere Zeta asked me to tell him about my life.

"There's not much to tell. I felt as if I never really knew my parents and they didn't know who I was."

"I'm sure you're right. If they knew who you really were and if you knew who they were, you all would have treated each other quite differently." I hesitated to speak. Ere Zeta said, "Go on, continue."

"Well, I was born in New York. We moved to Pennsylvania because my father had a hard time finding work. Then back to Brooklyn the summer before third grade. When I was in sixth grade my grandmother died and six months later my grandfather."

"Is that around the time Natalie disappeared?" He asked.

I didn't remember having mentioned that to him, or anyone.

"Yes, her family moved away. I never saw or heard from her again. My parents moved to an unfriendly place. My mother got sick and she died."

"Darci, you're marking your existence by all the difficult things that have occurred in your life. Give yourself a break; celebrate Our Lady of Mercy. Have mercy on you, forgive yourself for judging those experiences and let them go. They'll complete themselves. Surround and fill yourself with the Light of Spirit."

"How do I do that, Ere Zeta?"

"It's a process of visualization. Everyone has his own twist on it. You can close your eyes and imagine your spiritual heart; take a moment to center yourself, breathe the loving in and out. See white Light coming from the highest, holiest realms. A Light shower, a solid column, radiance, energy—it doesn't matter. Just move into it and always ask that the Light be present for the highest good. Spirit will handle the rest."

In the days to follow we walked through vineyards crimson and gold, past velvet hills that looked like dyed, sheared wool; through olive orchards with branches growing out of gnarled tree trunks; by the harbor and the beach with the sea lapping at the soles of our feet and Ere Zeta's words lapping at the very soul of my being. He spoke to me of Jesus and the Disciples, of Lao Tse and Buddha, of infinite Light and love and forgiveness. I was in something like a heightened state whenever Ere Zeta was near me. My skin tingled, my breathing slowed, my heart opened to a greater loving than I had ever known. If the summer was one of delight and aliveness then autumn was the season of my transformation, the season of my awakening into the Light.

Fourteen

February 14, 1961

Dear Dad,

Hi, hope this card finds you in the best of health. I've been in Madrid since November, living near the university and doing well in my classes. I'm working as a docent, a sort of tour guide, taking groups through the Prado Museum. It's filled with amazing art. Goya, Velazquez, El Greco—he's from Crete like grandma. I'm grateful she taught me Spanish!

Love, Darci

P. S. photo is my favorite painting, Las Meninas by Velazquez

꙳

"Darci love, it is awesome, painted in sixteen hundreds. He is master of light and shade. I can see why is your favorite painting."

"And you're my favorite person, Olivia. I'm so happy you're here."

Olivia dabbed the tip of my nose with her finger, stuck her tongue in the little space between her teeth and told me there was a poet, Raphael Alberti, who had dedicated a poem to the painter of *Las Meninas*. "I think I remember," she said, slowly shutting her eyelids like small seashells. She stood several feet back from Velazquez's magnificent baroque canvas depicting the golden haired child, Princess Margarita, surrounded by her maids and friends with the reflection of her parents, King Philip IV and Queen Mariana, in a rear mirror and Velazquez himself painting in the background, and shared the poem.

> *"Life appeared one morning*
> *and begged him*
> *Paint me, paint my portrait*
> *as I really am or as you would*
> *really like me to be.*
> *Look at me, here, I am a passive model,*
> *still, waiting for you to capture me.*
> *I am a mirror searching for another mirror..."*

꙳

We left the Prado, walked down the grand avenida. I turned to Olivia, "I wish you could stay with me but my room near the university is tiny, impossible, as my grandmother used to say about her small garden."

"No, my aunt would not hear of it if I do not stay with her when I come to Madrid."

We passed stores, banks, hotels, restaurants and lovely old churches, walking leisurely as if it were a mild spring day. In truth it was the last week of February and cold.

"Darci love, you are natural in Madrid. You fit in with the *Madrilenos*. They love to dress up and stroll," Olivia said, looping her arm around mine.

We walked through a public square with an impressive tiered fountain, water flowing from the top to the middle to the bottom level. We turned a corner and came to a modern apartment building. Laundry hung across the apartments' small balconies like so many white birds perched high on wires, ready for flight. But they weren't birds and with laundry hanging from every floor the five-story building appeared seedy.

We arrived at her aunt's apartment. Olivia said, "I brought for you beautiful clothes from me, is okay with you?"

She handed me a box.

"Olivia, I used to get my clothes from my cousin May in paper bags. I can't believe you...wrapped in tissue paper in this ritzy box. The pink suit! I remember you wearing it the day we met on the plane."

"Yes, I remember also."

"Silk, linen, is it okay with me? Does the Prado have art?"

᠊ᴥ᠊

Olivia and Michael visited several times over the next three years. They took me to England to see the musicians Michael had fashioned his hair after. The band had a new drummer, Ringo Starr, and had changed its name to the Beatles. We sang *I Want To Hold Your Hand* all the way back to Spain. Although I didn't have the opportunity to meet with Ere Zeta again, I did dream of him, and along with my academic studies, I read his prolific writings on the human condition and what he calls "the spiritual promise." While my professors spoke to my intellect, Ere Zeta somehow spoke to my heart and recalled my soul.

Fifteen

I was at the University of Madrid in Spanish Lit reading *Don Quixote* when I learned of President Kennedy's assassination. Later in the day and still in shock I contacted Olivia. She didn't have time to talk and she didn't call back as she promised she would. I began to realize that she was less available. We were living in separate cities, each with full lives and though it gave me reason for pause I didn't dwell on it.

During the summer I received a disturbing letter from my cousin May. Our mutual friend, Andrew Goodman, who attended Queens College with May, had been killed. With Michael Schwerner, another white New Yorker and James Chaney, a Negro from Mississippi, Andy had volunteered to help Negroes in the South register to vote. All three had been murdered. In my mind I saw them bathed in white Light, and beyond the pain in my heart I had a sense that my sending Light for the highest good was helping their souls to make a transition. Still the pain was tremendous. I called Olivia and once again she was unavailable.

"Michael, I haven't spoken to her in months. She doesn't call me anymore. What's goin' on?"

He cleared his throat as if to clear the way into uncharted territory. "Darci, things have changed. Olivia's not here with me, she's left."

"She's left—where to?"

"Right now she's in Athens."

"But I had no idea, we were so close."

"I had no idea either," he said with a trace of sorrow in his voice.

"Can I call her?"

"She doesn't want to be contacted now and I'm honoring that."

"How are you, Michael?"

"This is as rough as it gets. We didn't have traditional 'as long as we both shall live' marriage vows. For us it was as long as we both shall love."

"I'm sure she still loves you."

"Perhaps, but she's not *in* love with me. Darci, you don't usually call just to chat. What's going on?"

"A friend from Queens, Andy Goodman, he was murdered."

Michael took the time to explain to me that no one dies without the high self coming into agreement with the soul and that this was also true of Andrew. In the midst of his own troubles Michael was living the teachings of Ere Zeta.

"I don't get it, Michael. Andrew was as good as they come and you're a saint. Why does this stuff happen?"

"It's the way things are here."

"In Spain?" I asked, dazed.

I could almost hear him smile as he gently said, "No, on the planet. You think if you have a tragedy or a hard knock that's it, you're through. Kennedy's a perfect example. You know he had an older brother killed in the war? You think because the president's been killed, his family'll never have another hard knock? I doubt it."

"But it shouldn't be that way."

"Be careful, you're 'shoulding' on yourself."

"Very cute, Michael. Listen, I think I'm gonna visit my dad. It's been a long time. He's only written twice. And we've only spoken a few times."

"If you go over Christmas, I have two tickets. I'm going to see my mother. You can come here and we'll travel together," he offered.

"Yeah, school's out, it would be a perfect time."

⚘

The months ticked away like minutes. Before I knew it school was in recess and I was in Barcelona. We greeted each other with hugs.

"It's so good to see you, Michael."

"And you, Darci. You must be exhausted."

"I am. I haven't slept much. I've had exams all week."

"Come on, I'll take your bag upstairs; we'll have plenty of time to catch up on the flight."

I followed Michael up the curved staircase to the third floor.

"This room is even more lovely than I remembered."

"Rosa lit a fire for you before she left."

I crossed the room, glanced at the four-poster bed with its layers of white linen and warmed my hands in front of the stone fireplace. Michael stoked the fire. The flames crackled; elongated shadows moved on the walls.

"How is Rosa?" I asked.

"Fine, she only comes in two days a week now. I really don't need her more."

"Your annulment is final?"

"Last month... good night, Darci"

"Michael, don't go, please, stay and talk to me for a while."

"We have to be up very early tomorrow," he said.

"I know but I've been lonely."

Michael smiled nervously. The crooked slant of his mouth that I'd always considered rugged seemed seductive and appealing, sexy. I had never thought of Michael as sexy before. I had never thought of him as anything other than Olivia's husband. A jumble of thoughts raced through my mind. Olivia was the sister I never had. I could tell her everything. She was my dear friend. I missed her. I hadn't been hugged or held since I last saw Olivia and Michael. I'd dated a few young men but I had not been intimate with anyone in the three years since Africa. I could hear Ere Zeta's words, 'when in doubt don't,' but I was twenty-one and a half and horny. I let Olivia's flight from our lives and the annulment of their marriage reinstating Michael to bachelorhood override my doubt. In that moment, under drowsy lids, my green eyes shamelessly beckoning Michael, it didn't seem to matter to me that I had only known him as Olivia's husband.

There was a thick rope of silence between us. He tugged at his end, I at mine and we met in each other's arms. We kissed. We didn't say much. We were both hungry for physical contact, for affection. Michael spent the night with me in his guestroom. I felt him stirring at first light and while dawn whispered to the Mediterranean of mornings coming, we were with each other in ways I could never have imagined. Then playful as children, attentive as new lovers, we showered together, made the bed, drank from the same cup of coffee and left for New York.

"Your dad doesn't know you're coming?"

"I haven't told him, it'll be a surprise."

"Some surprise, you'll give him a heart attack."

"Nah, he's like an ox. You'll meet him, big thick neck, broad shoulders, deep voice."

"My mom's a nice woman. I want you to meet her, too."

"After your dad died, your mom moved to New York?"

"Moved back, she was from New York originally."

"My cousin May knows I'm coming. I'm gonna stay at her place in Greenwich Village. She calls it her 'pad'." I rolled my eyes. "We plan on skating at Rockefeller Center. My dad'll come to watch and you bring your mom."

"Sounds good," he agreed.

Sixteen

May's pad on Bleecker Street was in the middle of all the Village hubbub. There was so much activity on the street below whatever the time it was a wonder we slept at all.

"Dar, get up." May shook me. "It's ten o'clock, you need to leave already." She was still adorable, dimples, yellow curls, big blue eyes. May had been in my life for as long as I could remember. A year older than me she was at the opposite end of the spectrum from her mother, my father's older sister. If Aunt Anna was a pale lemon sourpuss then May was a cherry red sweet pie. My aunt was tight lipped as a pecking chicken. My cousin was loose as a goose.

I stumbled into the bathroom and showered with hanging baskets of showy philodendron that grew toward the small window, verdant leaves shiny from the water's mist.

"Wanna smoke some weed?" she asked as I came through the beaded doorway curtain into the all-in-one eat, sleep and live in room with dark wood floors.

"No thanks."

"It's good weed."

"I'm sure it is. I don't smoke grass."

"Why not?" she asked simply.

"I've been studying mystical teachings, May. I've learned that marijuana… it attacks your etheric body."

"Etheric body? You believe in that shit?"

"I do, and I'm surprised grass hasn't opened you up beyond your five senses."

She shrugged her shoulders. "Yeah, in that respect…"

"Then keep open to new information. Check it out," I suggested.

"Well what about it?" she asked.

"It's like paper being ripped. Because the etheric body's been damaged, your life energy pours out instead of flowing gently. I have a teacher who can see these things in a person's aura."

"Man, that's pretty far out."

"Yeah, more way out than marijuana. When you're turned on to the Light and Spirit it's the real deal. It's an inner trip to universes without end."

"Groovy bell bottoms, aren't you in style," she chided.

"You know, Europe's not in the dark ages anymore," I countered.

I took the F train at West Fourth to Continental and Seventy-first Avenue. The Q65A bus through the exclusive Forest Hills neighborhood with its aristocratic Tudor style homes on manicured parcels of land small as postage stamps, down Jewel Avenue past garden apartments and the government-supported housing project. There I was in front of the red brick building. It didn't seem imposing anymore, just older. I still had my key. I used it to gain access into the chilly vestibule, stopping first at the rubber mat to stomp the slush off of my pointy-toed boots. I decided not to ring the intercom. I wanted to go straight to my father's sixth floor apartment. I rang the doorbell; an eye looked through the peephole. The door opened slowly, but it wasn't my dad. A friendly looking woman who appeared to be in her late forties smiled and said, "Yes."

"I'm Darci," I said as if I was asking.

"Darci, I should've known, come in," she said putting me at ease. "Pini," she yelled to my father. "Pini, you won't believe it."

My father appeared and like the building he didn't seem imposing either, just older.

"Oh my God, as I live and breathe," he bellowed. "Look at you, all grown up." He hugged me and I could feel his tears against my face. "Darci, this is Arlene. We're gonna get married."

My father was happy. He was shoving questions at me right and left, while Arlene was shoving food at me.

"Have a banana. You want some sour cream and sugar with it? I'll cut it up for you."

"Thanks, Arlene. Maybe later."

"So when did you get in?"

"Yesterday, Dad."

"Yesterday! Where did you sleep?"

"At May's. . . "

"Darci, you wanna apple?"

"No thanks, Arlene."

"You heard about Andrew Goodman?"

"Yes, May wrote me."

"They should string the KKK bastards upside down by their balls."

"Darci, maybe you want some soup with matzoh balls?"

"Arlene, could I have a glass of water?"

"Of course sweetheart, you want ice?"

"Thanks."

"You gonna ice skate with May like old times?"

"You must be a mind reader, Dad. We talked about Rockefeller Center, it being Christmas and all."

"The skates are in the closet right where you left them." My father gestured toward the hall closet and I imagined my ice skates dangling next to the winter coats above the galoshes, across from my mother's wooden ironing board and the ancient Hoover vacuum cleaner. In that moment I looked down and realized that the twined fringe at the bottom of the rose sofa wasn't lying on the carpet. Apparently Arlene had taken over sewing up the fringe.

"Darci, Pini, a little sandwich?"

"Honey, I'll have a sandwich." My father made eyes at his betrothed. And his acceptance of her food offer made Arlene a very happy woman.

Seventeen

Manhattan was resplendent, dressed to celebrate Christmas. The soaring tree at Rockefeller Center seemed to reach the very juncture of heaven and earth. May and I glided over the ice while Aunt Anna, Uncle Ben, my father and Arlene swaddled in wool scarves, hats and gloves watched us and waved, huddled and talked, cold air vapors blowing from their mouths.

"So, is this Michael a boyfriend?" May asked, then turned a figure eight.

"A very good friend."

"How good?"

"He's like family to me."

"Like kissing cousins," she teased.

"I guess we are a lot more than friends. Oh, there he is now."

"Mmm. . . good looking, broad shoulders, square jaw—my

kinda guy," May purred.

I skated over to the far end of the plaza. "Hi, Mrs. Drummond. Hi, Michael."

"Hello dear," she said.

There was a strong resemblance mother to son. Light brown hair curled around the outside of Mrs. Drummond's fur hat. Michael's hair was the same color only straight. They both had the same deep blue eyes and small narrow nose. Mrs. Drummond's was a little bulbous at the tip. Michael's was chiseled perfectly. The arched shape of their eyebrows was the same and they both had porcelain skin, almost as if they had no pores. He wasn't as white as his mom... the Mediterranean sun I thought. And they weren't built alike. Mrs. Drummond was a petite woman.

"I'll meet you over there by my family." I pointed.

He gave me a little nod and his usual crooked smile.

When I approached, I heard Aunt Anna say, "Mary Alice."

"You know each other?" I asked. Just then my father turned around and went white as new fallen snow. "Dad, this is my friend Michael and his...." Mrs. Drummond was turning away.

"Pini, whatsa matter? You look like you saw a ghost," Arlene said.

"Okay so you know each other, from where?" Michael asked no one in particular.

"Michael, this is a mistake," his mother whimpered, tugging at his red plaid lumber jacket sleeve.

"Did you say Mary Alice?" I asked my Aunt.

My uncle Ben, standing next to her, began twitching profusely. My aunt stared at me with her lips so tightly sealed they formed a thin straight line that said don't cross over.

I looked directly at Mrs. Drummond. "Mary Alice what? What was your maiden name?"

Michael answered for her, "O'Malley, Mary Alice O'Malley."

"I prayed this day would never come," Mary Alice whispered, barely audible with her gloved hand covering her mouth, her blue eyes to the ground.

"And I prayed it would," my father mumbled. "Michael, your mother and me were kids, still in high school when she was pregnant and we got married."

Like a hot iron pressed to my flesh his words branded me. I curled over like a wave and crumpled to the ground. Michael reached out to lift me but I recoiled and reacted like a child having a temper tantrum. I had left home after high school to discover who I am. What had I uncovered, a stranger, a dirty incestuous girl. While shame and panic clawed at me I cried, "Don't touch me, you're my brother." I untied the laces and left my ice skates right there on the ground. May gave me the saddest look anyone ever had. I grabbed my bag, put my boots on and didn't look back.

I walked for hours, feeling twisted and broken, numb to the cold and to the surroundings. The committee in my head held an ongoing meeting with my father, bitterly accusing him of my emotional demise, of perpetrating my shame. I beat my fists against his barrel chest and in biting, acrimonious language I castrated him so that he could father no more. Then like an animal gone off to lick it's wounds I entered into a desolate alley, sank down on my haunches and sobbed. I don't know how long I was in the narrow passage but it was the smell of urine that brought me to my feet. Close by, a vagrant was relieving himself against the wall. I left quickly and found myself in front of Saint Patrick's. Inside the vaulted cathedral, intoxicating pyramids of votive candles reminded me to call myself forward into the Light. *Lord God, I ask to be filled, surrounded and protected with your holy Light for the highest good.* I thought about all the prayers the candles represented. Some prayed for their heart's desire to come to pass; others prayed for things not to happen. I reflected back to how lucky I'd felt when I first met Michael and Olivia, and I remembered Michael telling me that coincidence was God working and remaining anonymous. I lit a candle adding my unspoken thoughts to the thousands that had gone before and wondered if the Light and God had forsaken me.

It was dark when I returned to Greenwich Village, but I couldn't bear to face my cousin. I stopped at one of the smoky crowded coffeehouses on McDougal and languished over a cup of hot chocolate that burnt my tongue. When I finally arrived at May's she was sleeping, her yellow curls spilling over the pillow. Disheartened that I was losing Michael as my lover and tormented that he was my brother and we had made love, I lay down beside my cousin in the double bed and escaped the insanity my life seemed to be.

⚜

Morning broke into my sleep bringing an early call. The telephone was on my side of the bed. I reached for it quickly, still not wanting to face May, and whispered, "Hello."

Michael's voice was strong, "Darci, please, let's meet. You don't have the full information."

"I'm so ashamed, I can't see you," I said.

I got up from the bed and walked a few steps into the bathroom with the telephone. I could hear him breathing.

"My mother and Pini explained it all to me," he said.

"I wish they could explain it all away."

There was an awkward silence. Then he said, "No one can do that, but we can choose how we're going to deal with it all."

"Michael, are you out of your mind, what's there to deal with. This is a nightmare."

"Darci, they were very young. My mother and John Drummond were high school sweethearts. He signed up for the army; my mother flipped out. She broke up with him, dated your dad for two months, got pregnant. She's Irish Catholic. Abortion was out of the question. Pini didn't abandon her. He did what he thought was the right thing. They married against his family's wishes. Your grandfather was despondent because she wasn't Jewish. He considered Pini dead, even said the mourner's prayer. Didn't see him for years. Did you know that?"

"Of course not, it was all a big secret."

"Pini and my mother stayed together almost a year and a half after I was born, but they didn't have money, they didn't have family support. Although your father said—"

"My father... he's your father too."

Michael continued, ignoring my interruption, "Pini said his mother visited once after I was born, but she was afraid. Her husband forbid it. Even when they divorced and Pini married Sela three years later, Harry Beriman didn't attend the wedding and he wouldn't allow your grandmother to go. John Drummond was there for my mother—for me, despite the circumstances. He married her... adopted me... with a family inheritance they moved as far away... to California. They did what they thought was right for those times. I couldn't have had a more loving, affluent childhood. I'll always consider him my father."

"Look, that's all well and good, Michael—but it doesn't undo the fact that we're brother and sister. We slept together...we did things."

"Ere Zeta is in New York," Michael said. He's at the Waldorf. If anyone can help. . . something else, your grandfather didn't see your father again until after you were born. Your mother sent baby photos of you to your grandmother. She left them out. Your grandfather saw them and wept. You were the one who brought the family back together. You know how Ere Zeta says there's a blessing in everything."

"Not in this mess," I said weakly. "I really can't talk anymore. Good luck, Michael."

I put the phone back. May was still sleeping or, thankfully, playing possum. I turned on the shower, took off my nightgown, sat down on the floor of the tub and cried. I thought about how my mother had penny pinched all those years so I could have the wedding she never had. The wedding my grandparents didn't attend. I missed my mother and I cried for all the sorrow and anguish in the world, but mostly I cried for myself.

Eighteen

"Excuse me, can you please call up to a guest?"

"Certainly, young lady. The guest's name?"

"Ere Zeta."

The gray-uniformed clerk at the registration desk tilted his head ever so slightly and asked, "Miss Beriman?"

"Why, yes," I answered with obvious surprise.

"The gentleman is waiting for you in the conference room on the fourth floor."

I thanked him and walked to the elevator shaking my head in amazement at how Ere Zeta was always with me. In my dreams it was as if he was there first waiting for me to fall asleep. Now when I most need guidance and support, he shows up in New York.

The conference room was only a few paces from the elevator. I could see Ere Zeta through the etched glass door. I knocked lightly and entered. It was a small meeting room dominated by a large crystal chandelier hanging above a handsomely carved cherry wood table and six matching high back chairs. Ere Zeta was seated at the far end of the table with papers spread out before him. He stood up and we embraced.

"Please, Darci." He pointed to the chair next to his.

I sat down, swallowed hard and with my eyes averted blurted out, "Why, why Ere Zeta?"

"That question, Darci, will kill off some universe. You can't have the answer on this level of existence and when you get to the next level that question will seem, well, mundane. The only worthwhile question is, 'Am I doing the best I can with what I know?' You knew what you knew, you did what you did and you cannot allow this to dictate the rest of your life. If you focus into this you'll beat yourself up to the death and you'll be right in the negativity."

"But the pain…" I groaned and tears streamed down my cheeks.

"It's a purifier, not a punishment. It's an opportunity to go from, 'oh my God, it hurts so much,' to, 'oh my God,' when you get above the pain. I can't take this from you, Darci. This is the flow of your karma. And you'll have to validate what I'm saying, see if it fits for you."

"But I feel like the Light's abandoned me."

"Never, it's always present. You have to call yourself forward into it."

"I have," I said hopelessly.

"But you're not able to partake of the Light. You have to open your hands and pull the energy of spirit toward you. And that means letting go of what you're holding on to. If you want to hold on to the story, the negativity, you have a right to it. The Light is in the value of the relations you have with people, not in how or why or the way it ends."

"Are you saying there's value in this?"

"Of course. It's all part of your path into Spirit. But it's difficult for you to know because there's so much distracting you. Out of God comes all things, that which you label good and that which you label bad. The keys to your awakening are being presented to you in every moment of your beingness. You haven't quite secured the level you're on, it's shaky. You want to fall back to your familiarity and that will kick you in the head. You were unhappy and uncomfortable with yourself for years. You didn't like it then and you are not going to like it now. You have to be bigger than your own life. You have to pull yourself above your dilemma. There's really nothing esoteric about it. Just handle this level as it comes. It takes great strength to be happy. By all means go inside yourself and awaken the inner strength...."

I sat silently while Ere Zeta's words quickened inside of me.

"Don't you think God knows the experiences you need in order to awaken?" he asked.

I nodded.

"But you're in darkness, damning the experience as not valid for you because it's not spiritual and you can't know Spirit because of the darkness."

I cleared my throat that had filled with tears. "Ere Zeta, you've said many times to love it all, but I don't know how to love this."

"Then just love yourself through it all."

I repeated, "Love myself through it all." A chill ran up my spine. When it reached the nape of my neck my head jerked in a tight, counterclockwise stir. "Love myself through it all. I suppose I could work on that." Thoughtful, I slowly rose. "Thank you, Ere Zeta for the teachings, for your loving."

We embraced again. I walked toward the elevator when I realized I hadn't told Ere Zeta how much I loved him. I turned back to the conference room, pressed my face against the glass to show I had a little smile, but I didn't see him. I looked right, then left. I opened the door. Ere Zeta wasn't in the room. I rode the elevator back down to the lobby and went over to the front desk to ask for a piece of paper and a pen. The clerk approached me with stationary and pen in hand.

"Hello again, Miss Beriman. This is for you. Mr. Ere Zeta said you would be wanting this."

"Thank you," I chuckled realizing that my teacher had vanished from the fourth floor conference room and had reappeared to the unsuspecting desk clerk, with instructions for my writing needs.

⚜

Beloved Ere Zeta,

Beyond thanking you, I want to say how deeply, how very much I love you. In Light,

Darci

⚜

I walked out of the Waldorf Astoria onto Park Avenue. Above, spectacular billowy white clouds floated across the sky and a long ago memory floated across my mind. I hadn't thought of Natalie in years. My childhood friend used to say that downy clouds were pillows filled with angel feathers. I heard her saying, "Look, Dar, the angels are pillow fighting." I was transfixed by my remembrance when I saw a blue sky opening in one of the clouds, shaped like a perfect heart. I placed my hands over my own heart and knew that the Light was in the value of my relationships and that it really didn't matter how or why or the way they ended.

I returned to my cousin May's. She was on the phone when I came through the beaded doorway curtain. She held her hand over the black mouthpiece and whispered, "It's your dad. Do you wanna talk?"

"Not right now," I whispered back.

"Uncle Pini, I'll tell her you called. Bye." May hung up the receiver. She looked at me with embarrassed sad eyes. "This is awful you and Michael finding out that you're brother and sister. You slept together, didn't you? I'm so sorry," she said.

"Don't feel sorry for me. I'm gonna be okay. I know now that no matter what's going on, no matter what it looks like, everything is all right."

We hugged and cried, and spent the next two days at the Metropolitan and Guggenheim Museums. Then I returned to Spain.

Part Three

Nineteen

"Miss Beriman, where may I find the *Las Meninas* painting?" he asked, reading my name tag.

I told the man standing at the information desk that I'd take him there, that it was my favorite.

"Thank you. You're fluent in English, Miss Beriman?"

He was cute, big shoulders, narrow waist, a well cut tweed jacket over a blue dress shirt, chino pants. I found him attractive and I found myself cooing, "Yes, from New York. Please call me Darci."

"I'm from Lexington, Kentucky, myself. I'm Kevin, Kevin DeMornay."

"Well here you are, Kevin."

"It's spectacular. I've waited a long time to see the original. Isn't this something, larger than I expected."

I stepped back, admiring his exuberance. His gentle brown

eyes had watered in the presence of Velazquez's masterpiece. He dipped his sandy, curly haired head into his hands. Then he covered his mouth as if no words could be uttered to express his awe and gratitude. He didn't try to impress me with his artistic critique. Kevin DeMornay was moved and he let his emotions show freely.

I returned to the information desk. When the Prado was about to close, Kevin came by. "What a gift—I'm overwhelmed by the works here." He paused as if to contemplate the paintings one last time. "Miss Darci, I'll be back. I look forward to seeing you."

"*Adios*," I said and waved.

The following morning I was looking through my closet for something to wear to the university luncheon. I came across the pink silk suit Olivia had given me. It was time to pass it on. I looked at the suit and thought how special our friendship had been and how much I still loved her. I sent her Light and was startled out of my reverie by the sharp ring of the phone. I picked up the receiver and said, "*Hola*."

"Darci Beriman?"

"Olivia," my own voice rang out.

"Yes, love, is me."

"Olivia, you're not gonna believe this. I was just thinking about you. I came across the pink suit you gave me when I first moved to Madrid."

"This is amazing, how we are connected across miles, years, even lifetimes," she said. There was a brief silence, then she asked how I was.

"I'm well, Olivia. Tell me about yourself."

She told me she had a daughter, Sophia—a gifted, exceptional child, three years old. Her husband was French; they were living in Paris. "I am happy. When Sophia is little older I plan to open boutique. Have you seen Michael?" she asked.

"I spoke to him recently, but I haven't seen him in a while;" I had followed my teacher's advice and had relinquished the story years ago. I wasn't going back into the negativity. I didn't tell Olivia that I'd slept with Michael. I did tell her of the amazing turn in our lives—that Michael and I learned we had the same father.

"My God, this is so crazy," she shrieked. "I cannot believe this. Life is a fantastic magic carpet ride... don't you think?"

"I do and I'm learning to ride it. The more I surrender and accept, the more I see the glory in it all. You might not know this, Olivia. Michael's traveling with Ere Zeta. He's devoting his life to the spiritual teachings."

"No, I didn't know. I have not spoken to him in years. Last time I saw him... in Barcelona at the house. I go to take some things they were precious for me. Remember the guest room, love?" she asked.

How could I forget, I thought.

Her voice was sweet as she said, "The white linens and down pillows, they were gift from my grandmother. So I go take them... also some things from the kitchen. It was loving....

Michael is such good person. It seems perfect of all the seekers, Michael is the one to work with Ere Zeta."

I wanted to know why Olivia had ended her marriage and had broken contact with me. I tried to bring up the subject, but I couldn't get the words out. Eight years of being out of touch with each other had left me hesitant to ask. She relieved me of my anxious curiosity when she said, "It was over, Darci—before I left. I was no longer in love. I was untrue to myself. I hid my feelings from Michael, from our families, from you. It was unfair to him. It was miserable. I was miserable…depressed."

We spoke for a bit longer and pledged to do so again. I glanced at the clock. It was eleven-thirty. I was running late. I showered quickly. My hair was long again, down to my shoulders. I pulled it back into a twist, put on a white linen dress, the straw hat I bought recently—a little lipstick and I was off to the university.

As I'm walking to my seat in the banquet hall I sense someone coming up behind me. I turn around and I'm surprised for the second time today. "Kevin DeMornay, what are you doing here?"

"You just got here," he said knowingly.

I raised my eyes and told him, "I had the most wonderful call… an old friend from Crete. She got me placed on my first dig. Haven't heard from her in years… we were very close at one time."

"It's always nice to connect," Kevin said.

"Funny, she used that word… said we were connected. What did I miss?" I asked.

"A welcome to the visiting professors."

"Oh my God—you're one of them."

He smiled and agreed, "I am."

"Well, then I'll welcome you personally, Professor DeMornay." I extended my hand. It seemed small in his large grasp. I knew I was very attracted to him, but I was still taken by surprise at the intensity of that initial touch. It almost caused me to *shudder.* Even after graduation, my life, at the University of Madrid these past seven years, had been filled with studying, learning, teaching, becoming a professor—and little else. Kevin Demornay, I'm hoping that's all about to change. Lingering in the experience for a few seconds more, my eyelids fluttered while I fought against closing them. When at last I removed my hand, Kevin remained standing close to me.

"You're representing the museum?" he asked.

"No, I work here at the university."

"I thought you worked at the Prado."

"I volunteer occasionally. The Prado has a special place in my heart."

"What do you do here at the university?"

"I teach."

"You mentioned a dig on Crete, you're an archaeologist?"

"Actually, a cultural anthropologist. I specialize in the study of ethnocentrism."

"That's a ten dollar word, Miss Darci."

"Yeah, but it's basic, ten cent prejudice... a group or culture thinks it's superior—its ways are the best."

"With all the differences in this world... must keep you pretty busy. My southern accent; all the traveling I do... sometimes I feel people are pokin' fun at me."

"What is it that you do, Kevin?"

"I'm an art historian."

"No wonder you loved the Prado."

"It's one of the finer temples of the muses," he responded.

I think I know this lanky, gentle man from a long, long time ago.

✻

That summer I saw Kevin DeMornay often—every day to be exact. When he returned to the states we corresponded frequently and in the spring when he accepted a position at New York University, I visited and stayed with him.

"I'm looking forward to meeting your family, Darci."

"You're in for quite a treat, Kevin," I remarked facetiously.

"You haven't seen your father in several years?"

"It's been seven... I haven't been back to the states. Of course I write. His wife, my stepmother, Arlene, is a doll. She answers the letters," I laughed. "Which is more than my dad ever did."

"Then you haven't seen your cousin May's kids either, huh?"

"I can't wait to see them. May's pretty... she always liked good looking men. I bet those kids are gorgeous."

Kevin said, "Even if they're not...."

"You're right, to me they will be...."

✻

We all met at Bobos in Chinatown. May came with her husband, Danny Stein, and their two children. They really were gorgeous, like their parents. May's mother, my Aunt Anna, was critical of the restaurant and irritable as ever. Aunt Anna's nervous twitching husband, Ben, was still good-natured and meek. "*Oy veh*" had become my uncle's habitual and persistent verbal tic. Dad and Arlene were celebrating their sixth anniversary. My father's dark pompadour like a molting bird had thinned and grayed considerably. Arlene was plump and pleasant. They looked good. They were happy together.

"Your father and his wife, they're like two peas in a pod," Kevin said assessing the situation perfectly.

It was a wonderful reunion, as if no time had passed since we last saw each other. My family was vocal, expressive; eating like always. Opinions passed across the table as easily as egg rolls and duck sauce. May's little girl slurped wonton soup while the baby nursed discretely under a blue cotton receiving blanket draped over May's shoulder and breasts. Kevin for all his southern gentility felt right at home.

Twenty

At Christmas Kevin and I met in Paris. The days were short and cold. The city was alive, in full swing. It was a magical, exhilarating time for us. We took an hour-long ride by train southwest to Chartres and had lunch in a charming fifteenth century restaurant on the bank of the town's meandering Eure River. I don't remember what we ate, but the table setting was a veritable garden of sunburst yellow and cobalt blue. Completely myself with Kevin, I picked up a small plate and turned it over to read the stamp on the underside. He puckered his lips and mouthed, "Limoges." I told him about my mother's weekly summertime forays to the movie house on Jamaica Avenue in Queens. For women like my mother the air-conditioned theatre was a reprieve from the New York heat and never-ending domestic chores. Rewarded for their patronage, they were given the opportunity for a minimal sum to purchase a dinner plate, a cup and saucer, a soup bowl. Ultimately to assemble a full set of matching dishes.

We walked to the historic Notre Dame de Chartres Cathedral, its two bell towers spiraling into the frigid wintry sky. Kevin remained outside the North Portal studying the sculptures and large statues of the prophets, patriarchs and angels. *Melchizedek. Saint John. Abraham. Solomon.* I went inside to warm up. I saw two old women dressed in black, on their knees circuiting a maze built into the floor. It was a labyrinth, its pattern different than the ones I'd seen years before on coins found at Knossos. It wasn't the intimidating labyrinth of the Minotaur.

Pensively I began to walk the sacred path. With each meditative step I forgave some transgression, real or imagined. I forgave my mother for dying. I forgave my father for his secrets. I forgave Michael for sleeping with me and myself for sleeping with him. I forgave Olivia for leaving me. I forgave myself for my judgments. With each utterance I brought myself to the altar of forgiveness and shattered some crystallization of arrogance, pride and ignorance that resided in me but did not serve me. No monster to run from. No urgency to discover myself. With each step of the labyrinth, with each breath of my life, who I am was being divinely revealed to me.

Upon our return to Paris we met with Olivia and her husband, Francois. Sophia was indeed a precocious child, Olivia even more beautiful than I remembered her. I was concerned about seeing Olivia but the passing of time had dulled the feelings of disappointment I held toward her and forgiveness had freed my heart. We were warm and friendly. We did not pick up where we had left off. It wasn't like that. It was just a get together with an old friend. We visited several of Kevin's friends as well.

"Kevin, I'm amazed at how many people you know in Paris."

"I went to boarding school in Switzerland. I still keep in touch with my classmates."

"Switzerland, that's a far cry from Kentucky."

"Not really there's lots of tobacco, thoroughbred horse money. Not all Kentuckians are Appalachian mountain people."

"I know more about Europe than I do about Kentucky," I said, embarrassed by my ignorance. "Honestly, I know Abraham Lincoln was from Kentucky, not a whole lot more."

"My family is old money, Darci, and lots of it. I was married by the time I turned twenty-two. Practically arranged... our families both owned champion racehorses. She was the first girl I was intimate with."

"The first time I had sex was during my summer on Crete. A student from Tanganyika, a young black man."

"Trying to shock me, are you?"

"For that I would tell you I had made love to my brother."

"With Olivia's ex-husband, Michael?"

"I didn't know he was my brother at the time."

"But Olivia was your friend."

"My good friend. She left, she was out of both of our lives. They split up. Their marriage was annulled. Maybe in some unconscious way it was the antidote for her leaving. I was lonely. We were both available."

Kevin took my hand and spoke slowly in a calm tone. "It must have been difficult when you found out."

"I was devastated. It was only Ere Zeta's wisdom that brought me back. He recommended that I love myself through it all, that I find the gratitude in the situation. It took me a while but I did." With childhood images forming on the lens of my mind I paused to catch my breath. "When I was a girl playing in my grandparent's basement I came upon a photo of my father with his first wife and their child. I wondered about that child. Where he was, how he was. I was wounded by the discovery that somewhere I had a brother. It was never spoken about in my family. Despite the circumstances I became grateful to have found my brother. What happened to your marriage?"

"It didn't last the year. I didn't love her... was a long time ago, some fifteen years." Kevin shifted to face me fully and said, "But I know I love you. I want to share my life with you."

This wasn't completely unexpected, but I was still taken aback. "With all you know about me?"

"Darci, you're a courageous, spiritual woman. I've just learned more from you about acceptance and living life as it comes than I could ever have imagined."

He paid the driver; we stepped out of the taxi. We were standing in front of the Eiffel Tower—it's woven steel graceful as Chantilly lace. Red neon light streaked across the sky. We were shivering in the sunset. Kevin held me close and whispered, "Marry me, be my wife."

Twenty-One

On July 6, 1973, two years after I first met Kevin, we were married on the cool lower slopes of the Himalayas in northern India. Garlands of red ginger and white orchids hanging from nine brass poles, representing the nine planets, encircled us. A red and gold veil covering my head and shoulders flowed loosely over my red sari. The Hindu priest, a small man dressed in white, chanted hymns and sat crosslegged on a large pillow. Using perfumed water and flame he invoked many forms of God to witness our union. We were barefoot, seated in low, red velvet, throne-like chairs with ornately carved arms and legs that resembled lion's paws. I sat to Kevin's left.

We fed each other a morsel of rice to symbolize our mutual affection. We offered rice to the brass pot of fire set on the low table before us. The priest explained that this was done to invite a blessing on the union of our hearts. He told us that we were like birds without wings, that the Vedic wedding sacraments would attach our wings; and that in partnership life's journey would be easier.

The priest stood and had us both rise from our low chairs. We looked up at the noon sun as a declaration that our devotion and love be as steadfast as the sun. Kevin looked at me, his gentle brown eyes moist with tenderness, and said, "I hold your heart. You are joined to me by the Lord of all creatures." Then Kevin walked behind me, placed his hand over my left shoulder and touched my heart. His slim body appeared fuller in the loose-fitting collarless beige linen shirt and trousers. He removed the *mala* of red ginger and white orchids from around his neck. I took off my long floral necklace and we exchanged *malas*.

"May my body be free from disease and defect and may I ever enjoy the blessing of your companionship," I said to my groom.

The priest chants *om shanti shanti*, takes a length of bright yellow cloth, raises one end of my floor-length veil; ties the two fabrics together in a knot and wraps the yellow cloth around Kevin's waist several times. Fastened to each other and barefoot, we walk around the fire. Sweet perfumed water is poured into our cupped hands. We sign the marriage contract promising our life-long commitment. *Om shanti shanti.*

Legions of young Indian women have signed similar contracts, their marriages arranged while they were still infants, never given the opportunity to choose their own partners. I wonder if Kevin and I have chosen each other or if life has chosen us for each other. *Om shanti shanti.*

✦

I had come to India to study the Hindu and Islamic practices of decorating their houses of worship. Unlike the stories of Hindu gods told through sculpture, Muslims were forbidden by their religion to carve the human figure. Kevin joined me for my summer research project. While we rode on the train through teakwood forests filled with towering trees that bore enormous leaves, and through tea plantations up the steep incline to the northeast city of Darjeeling, my mind traveled back to how my parents had given me a D name after a cup of Darjeeling tea they had fallen in love over. Now, thirty-one years later, my life had brought me to this city surrounded by hillside plantations where the exotic black tea grew. I thought about the unknown and the unknowable and how we really can't know what's coming next in our lives.

✦

Smeeta was my research assistant, my interpreter, my guide and my friend. Together we waded through a green sea, submerged to our thighs in tea plants. Heads wrapped open turban style in white cotton, tea pluckers were bobbing around us like small sailboats. Smeeta ran her brown hand across the top of the evergreens and I did the same.

"Here in the north," she said, "the plants grow slowly because of high altitude and cool air."

I nodded in understanding.

Smeeta said, "Professor DeMornay, slow growing tea has more flavor. Darjeeling is the finest."

I thought about Darjeeling tea all summer long. For me, India was about sacred cows, Hindu holy men and Darjeeling tea. India was noisy open-air market places, monsoons bringing relentless rain and Darjeeling tea. The highlights of my stay in India were the holy Ganges River with its beginning in an ice cave high in the Himalayan house of snow, the white marble Islamic tomb at Agra known as the Taj Mahal, and the Darjeeling tea.

Summer in India transitioned easily to fall and to my renewed life in New York. My career had exposed me to a plethora of cultures, religions and ideologies. I was no longer anti-ritual. In fact I regarded many rituals as benevolent and worthy of respect. Some I held in high esteem. At Saint Patrick's Cathedral, where years before in my agony I had questioned whether the Light and God had forsaken me, I took the sacrament of communion. At his last Passover supper, Jesus Christ blessed the matzoh and wine and said to his disciples, "Take, eat. This is my body, this is my blood. This do in remembrance of me." *And so I did in remembrance of him.*

I was no longer anti-New York. I was enjoying New York this second time around. I had come to know from my spiritual studies and my travels that wherever I go I take myself. I was determined not to set up patterns of defeat in my life and not to be a loser in my own fantasies.

⚜

"You changed your name?"
  "Yes, Dad."
  "To Darjeeling?"
  "Yes, Dad."
  "What, they brainwashed you in India?"
  "It's more like my *heart* was washed."
  "If it's all right with you, I'm still gonna call you Darci."
  "Sure, Dad."
Most people accepted the name change with ease. Some, like my cousin May, just called me Dar. Kevin loved the conversion. He looked at me with those gentle eyes and in his Kentucky drawl said, "Darjeeling DeMornay—sounds smooth as warm butter spread with a hot knife."
  And like drawn butter I melted into my husband's strong arms.

Twenty-Two

On a lazy Sunday morning while we loafed in bed reading the *New York Times*, Kevin stretched his long body like a cat and announced, "Darjeeling, we ought to celebrate your thirty-fifth with a photo safari. No research projects, no art trips, just a summer off to cut loose."

I took a sip of coffee from the cracked mug with the hand-painted sunflower I'd shipped back from Spain, ran my free hand through my husband's uncombed curly hair and beamed like a kid. Kevin took his reading glasses off, pushed the newspapers to the floor, reached over, cuffed my wrist with his large hand and drew me on top of him. Sixteen floors above Central Park, in our cavernous apartment filled with books, art and travel photos, as we had done on so many Sunday mornings before, we made love.

✻

Four months later we set out for the Massai Mara Game Reserve in Kenya. It had been ten years since I last corresponded with Africa. He wrote back that his wife, Aisha, knew only of our friendship as co-workers at the dig on Crete. In my follow-up letter I assured him it would remain that way. He was pleased to hear from me and once I convinced him that our past involvement in no way troubled my husband, he was of great assistance to Kevin in planning our trip. So after ten adventurous days in Kenya, I was looking forward to crossing into Tanzania—the country once called Tanganyika I'd heard so much about from my old friend. But nothing was easy on this continent and only months before, Tanzania had closed its borders to Kenya.

We awoke in the colorless pre-dawn mist. Kevin asked me to wear my hair back.

"How come? You never tell me how to wear my hair."

"So it doesn't blow into the flames."

"Into the flames—what are you talking about?"

"You'll see, just get dressed."

I knew Africa had arranged for us to take part in a game drive and that I would see him later in the day. But I didn't expect the experience that was to follow. While we drove to meet the sunrise, the stillness metamorphosed into hues of deep purple. What looked like a swollen mud village from afar turned out to be an enormous balloon.

Brown, our driver, explained, "not to frighten the animals."

One of the crew shouted to Kevin, "We're on. We expect the weather window to hold." Then to me, "Ma'm, you might want to wear your hat, the overhead burners are very warm."

"Happy birthday, Darjeeling."

"Kevin, you're a man after my own heart."

"And you, Darjeeling DeMornay, are following after a sheep, duck and I think a rooster."

"Uh huh, are you insinuating now that I'm thirty-five I'm old enough to have been around when the first balloon went up with that menagerie?"

Kevin looked at me again and clucked his tongue.

The crew loosened the ropes attached to the basket. We were launched, rising like hot air above the glorious Serengetti Plain. We were barely below the equator and I could see snow on the volcanic peaks of Kilimanjaro. We drifted above thousands and thousands of migrating wildebeests. Their exaggeratedly long faces, beards and humped backs made them look sorrowful. Perhaps they are…. This scourge they endure year after year. The drought with its parched land forcing them to move in search of green Savannah grass, predators at their hoofs, wide rivers that claim the old and weak, white-backed vultures wheeling above. This spectacle extended beyond the vista of our eyes. Kevin pointed out giraffe grazing on the thorny flat-topped acacia trees. We spotted zebra, impalas, elephants and hippos in the Seronera Valley.

I was still in a euphoric state when we landed and I caught a glimpse of Africa, his long legs, approaching. As he moved closer, his brilliant smile and twinkling eyes were unmistakable even though he had a mustache tracing his full upper lip and a goatee sprinkled with prematurely gray hair.

"America, it has been seventeen years!" he said with a look of astonishment coming onto his face.

We hugged close and long. Memories of the whitewashed guesthouse, my roommate Denmark, the wild fig trees and the beach flooded my consciousness. The lasting bond I had with my old friend went far deeper than the physical level. That hug and his body redolent with the scent of clove brought me back to my summer in the Greek islands.

Africa looked over my shoulder and said to Kevin, "I'm back on Crete at the dig."

"She's told me about Denmark, Mykonos, Dr. Evans and his perennial cigarette."

"Puffing on one coffin nail after another, that would be Dr. Evans."

Kevin smiled generously and shook his head lovingly. He and Africa took to each other with the traditional palm, thumb, palm handshake. I was with two extraordinary human beings—both, great men in their own right.

Twenty-Three

The next days were spent meeting Africa's delightful wife Aisha, five lively children and the extended Mbingo family. We were treated to delicious thick plantain porridge, sweet potato loaves, dramatic African tales and a trip southeast of the Serengetti Plain to the fossil beds of Olduvai Gorge where archaeologists Louis and Mary Leaky had unearthed evidence that the earliest human existence probably began in the Great Rift Valley of East Africa.

Then five days by ourselves on Tanzania's east coast. We drank *pumbe*, a local beer made from millet. We sunned on white sand beaches ringed with palm trees and we swam in turquoise waters. In the evenings we read, pleasured each other with our bodies, and watched the moon dip into the Indian Ocean.

＊

When we came back to see Africa on that last leg of our journey, his jubilant demeanor had turned somber, his twinkling eyes flat.

"America, Kevin...you know this land has a vile underbelly too."

"Sure, the poverty, history of slave trade...." Kevin answered.

"Can I take you somewhere?"

"Of course," I said, "we're yours until we go home."

We drove down yet one more long bumpy unpaved dirt road. The faded green structure looked too tired to be standing. A stench of urine and death hung on the building like a mourner's veil. I glanced at my husband with apprehension. He took my hand in his and squeezed it.

Africa spoke to us while he led the way. "They're orphans. The parents are being prepared for burial in this same building." He opened the ridiculous screen door filled with holes and said, "They crossed over the border searching for food... malaria... bilharzia." He understood my questioning expression; addressed it at once. "A parasite from contaminated water. Poachers came, killed the ones still alive who probably lay claim to the animals at the very watering hole that sickened them." He looked away and what he told us next unnerved and sickened me. "Wild hyenas came in the night. For some, only bones remained."

The children stared at us with big cow eyes. One little boy and girl were tied together at the wrists with string so it would be known they were brother and sister.

"Amadou, we can make a donation for food and medicine."

"Good, Kevin. I thought you would help out when you saw with your own eyes," Africa said.

I think we arrived at about noon. The three of us pitched in doing whatever was called for on a handle-the-most-urgent matters first, you're on your own, no one is supervising basis. We changed urine-soaked pads that lay atop the twenty or so cots that had been set up for the surviving children. While I sponge bathed scrawny limbed little bodies bloated with hunger, I envisioned each one bathed in healing white Light and I prayed for the Light to be with the children and with their deceased parents for their highest good.

Hours later, just before the sky began to darken, Africa asked us to wind down, to prepare to leave. "The jeep has been giving me some problems. I don't want to chance a breakdown, it's getting late," he said.

Four women working in the cornfield next to the dusty road stopped and waved as we drove by. They were all barefoot, tall and thin, in calf-length colorful dresses. Their hair was covered in the same print cloth.

That night Kevin and I were insomniacs. We hadn't complained about any of our accommodations, even when we slept in tents at the rugged Kenyan game reserve. Most nights we fell to sleep happily exhausted. Now we tossed and tugged at the blanket. We turned, rolled, pushed. We couldn't fall asleep and we couldn't console each other. We were haunted by the children—their pathetic eyes followed us into our sleeplessness.

"Darjeeling, we can do more."

"I know... that brother and sister...I can't get them out of my mind."

"God... I was thinking about the same kids."

"Kevin, do you ever want...."

"It would be nice to have a family."

"Adopted?"

"Sure, why bring more kids into the world. What a farce to think we're born with equal opportunity. Those kids face only the most dismal options...Jesus!"

"There's one way. We're all born with equal opportunity to know our own souls. Would you adopt the brother and sister?" I asked.

"I would," he answered.

I brushed lightly against his bare back. "Let's take another look—it's a big step. Our lives'll never be the same."

"And there's a lot to consider, Darjeeling, not just two sweet kids. Are you prepared to help them through this horrible loss, to raise children to adulthood, to have an interracial family?"

"Kevin, I learned a long time ago, there's only one race. It has many colors, but we all share one heart."

The hours wore on. When it was light enough, we returned to the fly-infested building. The horrific odors were as suffocating as the day before. One little girl with vacant eyes rocked back and forth, howling. It was explained to us that her brother had died in the night. I could not come to Africa and only delight in its wildlife and remote beauty. *Kevin and I were being called to something greater.*

The two that had been yoked by string were still alive, wide-eyed, lying on cots next to each other. The dehydrated girl perhaps four-years old, the boy curled in a fetal position about three. I sat on the edge of the cot with a spoon and a small bowl of *ugali* in my hands. She accepted the porridge eagerly, but kept watch over her brother to see if he was eating. Kevin had the sickly boy cradled in one arm while he patiently fed him the starchy *ugali*. The sister showing signs of fierce independence would try to wrap her skeleton fingers around the handle of the spoon, but she was too weak to do even that. The membranes inside of her little broad nose were so dry she could hardly breathe at first—sucking in the air through her parched mouth. Her teeny fingernails were brittle and ridged. Each line told a tale of famine and malnutrition. The children responded quickly. Within days we learned their names, Imani and Juma.

I held Imani close to me and I knew that *she was the child of my first intimacy*, conceived seventeen years ago when Africa and I were together. I recalled that long ago summer night on Crete when he asked, "Are you sure you want me to? My people say the first man you're with is the father of your first born, even if the baby comes many years after. They say the baby is hiding, waiting to be born later from a *bisisi*, a long pregnancy. It's said you have a *bisisi* child."

Imani is not the daughter of my womb, but she has waited and now this ebony girl is my true *bisisi* child born of a long *bisisi* pregnancy—born from the best part of who I am, born of my heart, of my loving. And yes, I am prepared to help Imani and Juma through the loss of their parents and to raise them to adulthood.

Twenty-Four

By weeks end we were able to bring Imani and Juma to the Mbingo house. Aisha Mbingo with her stunning angular face and Tanzanian reserve welcomed us as best she could under the newly crowded conditions of her home.

Kevin flew back to the states. First to New York to gather a dark blue suit, some shirts, ties, his Johnston and Murphy wing tip shoes and a pit stop to the barber. On to Washington D.C. to call in favors at the highest levels his family's influence reached. He wired me when he arrived in Washington. I received the telegram thirteen days later.

Africa who had followed in his diplomat father's footsteps was doing all that he could to facilitate passports and visas for Imani and Juma, for whom no birth certificates existed on a continent where nothing was easy, especially for Africans to leave.

I gave the children liquids and like fragile baby birds fallen from their nests I fed them small amounts in intervals around the clock until they gained strength and were able to take their meals with the Mbingo children. They had never used utensils.

"Juma, you will hurt yourself with the fork. Use the spoon like Imani," Aisha insisted. He put the fork down and picked up the spoon. "You are a good listener, Juma," she praised him. And his sweet face lit up.

I immersed myself in learning Swahili. All the while Imani and Juma were picking up English words from the bilingual Mbingo children. I learned to cook traditional dishes. Aisha laughed at me the first time I tried to make *ugali*. She said to her husband, "Amadou, this American girl needs strong arms." She gripped the wooden spoon. "Don't let it stick to the pot!" and stirred cornflower, water, milk and butter with the force of an Osterizer. I laughed too and put a pinch of salt into the large pot.

We hired attorneys in both countries. There were mountains of paperwork generated and seemingly insurmountable challenges to handle: death certificates for the parents, for the children proof of age, medical history, official change of name requests— *where no last name was known.*

Kevin came back to Tanzania to check on the children and me. The disfiguring bloat and the pasty complexions were no longer dominant. They were skinny, but much healthier. Juma even began to sprout hair on his little bald head and Imani's lips once cracked and caked with sores were turning smooth and plump. On the second night of Kevin's return, I slept twelve straight hours knowing that he would take care of the children. I awoke to the sounds of laughter outside. I went to the window and pulled the curtains back. Kevin had all seven children lined up playing Simon Says. At the moment I looked out all of the children were bent over touching their toes. Kevin only stayed with us for five days before he returned to New York for the start of classes in September. I took a leave of absence from my teaching position at Queens College.

When the children were well enough I dealt with getting them routine immunizations for entry into the United States. Finally we were in compliance with U.S. immigration requirements, and visas were issued by the state department. The children were under our guardianship while we petitioned the courts in the United States for adoption.

The night before we left, Africa asked me to bring the children outside. The four-bedroom ranch style house could have been a suburban number in any American neighborhood except that it was part of a walled-in compound. There was another smaller, but similar three-bedroom ranch house where Africa's parents lived. The six foot-eight retired elder statesman and his five foot-three wife tended the large vegetable garden. There were chickens and a coop, a smelly stable with several horses and a small pond stocked with fish. The sun had fallen silent two hours before and beyond the compound it was mostly dark.

"Imani, Juma, look up," he said in English. Then he pointed out the North Star and told them in Swahili it was at the end of the Little Bear's tail.

Juma frowned and asked, "What is a bear?"

Africa patted him lightly on the head and answered, "It's a large animal with shaggy hair. When you arrive to your new home in New York you will see big buildings that reach into the sky. It will be very different. Darjeeling will show you the North Star at the end of the Little Bear's tail and you will know you are under the same sky."

The children arched their necks and gazed at the wondrous light show above. I knelt down to their size and held them in my arms. Africa knelt down beside us and said, "She loves you both very much. She wants you to have a mother and a father. It would be good if you call Darjeeling, Mama and Kevin, Papi."

Twenty-Five

On November 16, 1976, Kevin, my father and Arlene, May and her parents awaited us at Kennedy International Airport in New York. My cousin and my stepmother held a huge hand-lettered banner that said, "WELCOME IMANI AND JUMA." Kevin scooped up the children, one in each arm. They called him Papi and planted kisses on his face that I swear have been imprinted on his countenance and have remained there always. Aunt Anna seemed somewhat annoyed as if she had just stepped into an elephant turd but then I realized we were in New York and as I remembered my pale gray aunt always looked as if she were sucking on a lemon. Besides, when we chose to adopt Juma and Imani, we knew our family would be met by some opposition. At the time of our decision we vowed to focus into the Light and to allow those who would be repugnant and antagonistic their darkness.

In preparation for Imani and Juma, Kevin had a wall in our apartment removed. Where once there were two guestrooms there was now one open bright space sporting a playful floor-to-ceiling mural of safari animals amidst thick-trunked baobab trees with foot-long fruit dangling from ropy stems, and thorny flat-topped acacia trees with Mount Kilimanjaro slathered in the background. The beds were done up with childlike animal prints, a teddy bear perched atop each. At the foot of each bed stood a long necked giraffe for hanging clothes. The windows were draped in sheer batik fabric with a colorful African motif.

The children sleep on and off. Me too. I get up, look in on them. Imani has the sweetest small heart-shaped face with a full upper lip that resembles a bow, reminding me that she is a gift from God. Her dark hair and skin are a healthy reddish bronze color. Her black eyes are almond-shaped, like mine. Juma's skin and hair also have that reddish bronze coloring. Juma's features are strong and broad like his sister's. I stand in the doorway as if in a dream. Sleepily I return to my bed, snuggle up to Kevin...sleep...get up again... peer in on Imani and Juma... lay down next to Juma, nuzzle my face against his little wooly head. During my five-month stay at Aisha and Amadou Mbingo's I slept in the same room with the children. Now I get up from Juma's bed and cuddle with Imani. I love her little girl smell. I breathe her in.

The next evening we brought the children up to the roof. With smiles spreading across their faces they both easily identified what Imani called, "The big star on Little Bear's tail." After my father and Arlene took them across the way to Central Park's Wildlife Center, Juma burst in the door. "Mama, I see real bear!" When a Goldilocks and the three bears float passed along Fifth Avenue where we were standing at the Macy's Thanksgiving Day Parade Juma squealed with delight. Imani shouted, "Look it's Little Bear, he came down from the sky."

I took the children to see Santa Claus at Macy's. We entered the huge department store from 34th street. The store windows displayed scenes from *The Miracle on 34th Street*, the movie about a Macy's Santa Claus who persuaded the court he was the real, plump, red-suited, white-bearded old man who delivered presents to good children at Christmas time.

"Mama, why you cry?" Imani asked.

As my eyes filled with water I was a child again being told by my mother that Santa Claus was a figment of the Christian imagination.

If Christmas in Manhattan dazzled the children, springtime liberated them. They loved to play barefoot in the grass at Central Park. Imani learned to tie her laces almost immediately. Juma was more creative, sometimes tying both little sneakers together. They'd take off their socks, roll them neatly, set them in a row and fling their sneakers as far as they could. Then they'd run and tumble and fall across the grass and retrieve them— squealing and laughing the whole time. Their little feet slapped the dewy blades of grass and made a sloshing sound. Imani would run back to the bench where I was sitting and report earnestly. "Mama, the grass is crying." I'd tell her they were surely tears of joy, the grass was so happy she and Juma were visiting again. She'd lower her small heart-shaped face to the ground reflecting on what I'd said, then raise up with an endearing smile. I'd smile, we'd look at each other and she'd pad back to Juma—the grass sloshing beneath her feet.

Exactly one year from the children's arrival in New York the adoption process was finalized. To mark the occasion we attended a performance of the International Afrikan American Ballet. Kevin got us second-row orchestra seats at Klitgord Auditorium in Brooklyn. Imani tugged at my dress when she saw how close up we were. I was aware that like me she understood this was a privilege. Kevin blew a kiss at me across Juma and Imani who were sitting between us and said, "Thank you, Darjeeling... thank you for our family." I saw the beginning of the mesmerizing dance and drumming through a curtain of tears.

We kept a two-sided easel permanently stationed in the children's large sunny room. They painted together sharing colors and brushes. Unlike other siblings they never argued. Imani watched over Juma like a mother hen. She would paint huge orange sun balls. On the other side of the easel Juma's paintings were lyrical from early on.

"Imani, please read me *Curious George*," Juma entreated his sister. Stomach down, skinny legs bent at the knees, ankles crossed in the air, Imani spread across her bed and read to her little brother while he painted away.

I didn't go back to teaching. The children thrived. They did well in school, music, art and sports. Juma asked endlessly to visit the polar bears at Central Park while Imani asked, "Mama, tell me how I'm your special girl?" And I would answer, "You're my *bisisi girl*... you waited to be born from my heart." I'd look at my daughter and it made all the sense in the world to me that my first-born child was a dark-skinned beauty. When the barber refused to work on Juma's hair, Kevin switched to a shop in Harlem where both father and son could have their hair cut together. Kevin was determined the children never lose their mother tongue and as a family we often spoke in Swahili. Decembers in our home were a cornucopia of grace and blessings with the celebration of Kwanzaa, Christmas and Chanukah. I never did get that Chanukah bush my father promised me as a child, and Kevin was right when he said, "Darjeeling, your eyes are as green and bright and as big as the tree... if you ask me you're getting off on this more than the kids."

I even hosted a Passover *seder* one year when May called and asked, "Dar, would you? I can't fit everyone." May and Arlene did most of the cooking. Ere Zeta and my brother Michael were in town. The table stretched from here to forever.

Imani seated next to May's daughter, Riva, named after our grandmother, turned to her blue-eyed cousin and said, "See my new ring... it's tanzanite from Amadou in Africa."

Yeah, purple—it's cool... I like it," Riva answered.

May's little boy said, "I have to pee."

And his mother said, "So go, quickly."

May asked Ere Zeta about the significance of the holiday. He looked down the length of the table like a camera with a zoom lens. His head turned slightly from side to side, his eyes made contact with everyone present and he said, "For those who are Jewish this comes out of your tradition. For all of us this comes out of our heritage. The *seder* is about a deliverance from bondage into freedom. It represents the spiritual journey from darkness into Light. Passover is about enduring to the end into spiritual liberation. It's a symbol of man's inner journey."

I scanned the room; saw Michael with his mother Mary Alice on one side, our father, Pini and Arlene next to him on the other and I had a glimmer of what Ere Zeta meant when he taught that those who endure to the end, win.

Twenty-Six

My precious boy was eight, his sister nine, when speaking for both of them he said, "Mama we want American names."

"But Juma, your names are special, they were given to you by your African mother and father."

"Mama." Imani swiveled with her hand on her hip like a runway model. "We'll keep them for middle names."

"I don't know... I have to think about it."

"Mama, please," they begged.

When I brought the subject up with Kevin, at first he covered his mouth, then he broke out laughing right in my face. "Correct me if I'm wrong," he kept on laughing, "but isn't their mother the well known Darjeeling DeMornay, queen of the name change realm?"

"How'd I get so lucky to have you as my husband?"

"You're the one who always tells me there's no coincidence!" he answered.

The children picked their own names. Our daughter became Wendy Imani DeMornay; our son, Gregory Juma DeMornay. I really liked their names. They fit them well.

One night after dinner we were up on the roof when Gregory, holding back tears, his lip quivering, said, "There's this kid at school—he's mean. He says I'm an alien…Wendy too—cause we don't look like you."

Almost two decades had passed since my friend Andrew Goodman was murdered during the Freedom Summer of '64. Since then I'd had plenty of practice in girding my heart against the stares and occasional sneers aimed at my family. Still, a sinking feeling came over me, the one reserved for mothers when their children are hurting.

"Do you remember Kunta Kinte?" Kevin asked.

"From Roots?" Gregory asked.

"Yes, Kevin answered.

"I remember," Gregory said.

"Me too," Wendy said with a puzzled look.

Kevin placed his large hands gently on Gregory and Wendy's shoulders and said, "When Kunta was a baby and his father named him he held him up to the heavens and said behold the only thing greater than yourself."

We all looked up at the clear night sky.

"Always remember the truth of who you are," Kevin said.

"We will Dad," Gregory said.

Wendy smiled and nodded in agreement.

⁂

A year later at dinner, Gregory, ever the spokesperson for change, asked us, "Can we have our own rooms?"

Kevin put his fork down and asked, "Won't you be lonely?"

"Mom, Dad," Wendy said, "We'll visit just like we always visit you for stories and hugs."

And so a wall went up again. Wendy's room housed the bookshelves, Gregory's the easel. Over the next few years the giraffes, mural and African theme made way for rainbows and teen idol posters in our daughter's room and sport's paraphernalia in our son's.

It was right about that time my father began addressing me as Darjeeling. Of everyone, I loved hearing my father call me Darjeeling. I felt as though he was finally acknowledging my choices. My father never voiced his opinion with regard to the children's adoption. He was a good grandfather. Wendy and Gregory meant the world to him and as he had done with me he regularly took them to New York's free and affordable cultural events. When he accompanied Wendy and Gregory if anyone stared at them he stared back. After all, my father still had to be right.

Instead of a Bar Mitzvah to celebrate Gregory's thirteenth birthday Kevin and I opted for a family trip to Tanzania.

"It's nice for Gregory to return and see where he came from, Darjeeling."

"That's good thinking; thanks, Dad."

"We'll help in anyway we can," Arlene added.

"Mom, I'm nervous about going back. I don't feel African. I mean I know I'm black but I'm American."

"I understand your feeling nervous, Wendy. You are American and you're also African, not only because you're black, because you were born in Africa."

"I remember fishing in a pond with John Mbingo. How old do you think he is now?" she asked.

"John's the oldest, about five years older than you. I guess nineteen."

"I don't remember the Mbingos, I don't remember Africa."

"You were little more than a baby, Gregory."

Our trip never came to pass. A severe outbreak of malaria in Tanzania kept us from going. Instead at Gregory's urging we went to Disney World in Orlando, Florida. Gregory remembered an earlier family trip to Disney World and he very much wanted to return. The first time we went Gregory was seven years old. There's a framed photo in our living room sitting on top of the baby grand piano, that both children play, of Mickey Mouse, one arm around Wendy who's clutching a Minnie Mouse doll to her chest, the other arm around Gregory who has a huge toothless smile.

⚜

Once a neighbor asked, "Don't you think those kids will have an identity crisis?"

"Probably," I answered. "I had to cross an ocean and back to find out who I was. With a mother like me I suppose so."

In actuality they always seemed to know who they were. As a teenager Wendy, who went through 'hair stages' having plaited, braided, straightened, relaxed, Afro'd and gone natural, answered my concern with, "Mom, my hair is about style. I'm about making a difference in this world."

Seeing Gregory's hair in dreadlocks for the first time, my father asked him, "What are you—a Rasta-Jew...you have yid-locks?" Gregory, guzzling a Pepsi after football, whirled around the kitchen trying to hold in a mouthful of soda until finally he couldn't contain himself any longer. He sprayed the room with Pepsi and lay down on the floor, delirious with laughter. I knew then that my son would walk through his life in humor and wisdom, hopefully claiming his place in the brotherhood of mankind.

And indeed it looked like Wendy might make a difference in the world. She was a well-rounded girl: A-plus student, marching band, senior class president and still she found time to read to those without sight at The Lighthouse for the Blind.

⚜

Gregory is his father's son. Having majored in art he opened a gallery in Soho. He specializes in Caribbean, African-American art. He has a great eye and he's building quite a following of patrons. His own talent lies in sculpting, with works reminiscent of the extraordinary Makonde carvers who live in Tanzania near the Mozambique border. Gregory was commissioned to do several sculptures for the Broadway show *The Lion King*. That's how he met Sandra. "A fine specimen of a young woman if ever I did see one," is how Kevin describes her. Leggy with a small waist and bubbly as a glass of champagne, Sandra is the consummate showgirl and a welcome addition to our lives.

Wendy always the scholar went on to Yale University School of Medicine.

Gregory's wedding was a phantasmagoric scene. Most of his wife Sandra's Broadway co-performers arrived at Tavern on the Green in full *Lion King* stage makeup and costume. Hakuna Matata was the greeting on everyone's lips. Everyone from Aisha and Amadou Mbingo, Sandra's family from the Bahamas, the 'old money' DeMornay family from Lexington, the New York Beriman clan to Kevin's NYU colleagues and the life-long friends he'd made years ago at the Harlem barber shop. In from Europe my brother Michael, and Ere Zeta who officiated the ceremony telling the young couple, "It is the energy of love you recognize in one another that brings you together this day. The purpose of marriage is so that you can learn from each other. So you can come into a higher expression."

⚜

Upon completing her residency specializing in contagious diseases, Wendy moved to Africa. Shortly afterward I received the following e-mail:

Mom,

I found out that a bisisi-child is born from your first sexual encounter. Did you have an affair with Amadou? How come you never told me?

Love you,
Wendy

I thought about my omissions and about my father's long-ago secret, and I imagined that all parents face the dilemma of telling their children either too little or too much.

I replied:

Wendy Doll face,
It was hardly an affair. We were teenagers. Besides, mothers don't usually tell their daughters things like that.
Love and Light, Mom

Her most recent e-mail was of a more serious nature:

Dear Mom,
I'm having a discouraging day. The AIDS epidemic is staggering here in South Africa and it's getting worse. Please send lots of Light to this part of the world. We need it. Love to Dad.
Your bisisi girl, Wendy

Twenty-Seven

This past summer Kevin headed up an art restoration project at a Byzantine church near Palaiochora on Crete. It was my first return trip to the Greek Island in forty years. I took Kevin to the writer Nikos Kazanzakis' gravesite. He asked me if I knew what the inscription on the granite stone read.

I told him, *"I am afraid of nothing, I want nothing, I am free."*

He sighed and raised his face to the sun. He was still handsome, my husband, with his head of curly white hair.

We rented a furnished bungalow overlooking the sea. A few days into our stay, I arose later than usual. Kevin was gone, off to the Byzantine church to restore fourteenth century icons. A pot of freshly brewed coffee and a sky filled with storm clouds awaited me. I passed on the coffee and pulled on my gray sweats so that I could head on down to the beach before the rain came. As I stood at the edge of the sea an avalanche of frothy waves advanced toward me, the breakers farthest away shooting spray into the sky like a chorus line of a thousand dancing fountains. A colony of whitish-gray, long-billed terns lifted off the sand, headed into a thermal and without flapping their extended wings, they glided gracefully like a band of angels called toward heaven.

A sudden violent gust of cold wind had me turning around and heading back to the bungalow. As I neared the white bungalow the blowing squall became a downpour of rain. I galloped up the steps to the porch, opened the sliding glass door and hurried inside. I was about to pour myself a cup of coffee. The phone rang. I picked up the receiver and panted, "Hello."

"I'm surprised to hear from you, Michael. What's up, everything okay?"

Michael spoke slowly articulating each syllable. "Darjeeling, I wanted to let you know that Ere Zeta has passed over."

I closed my eyes and gulped, "Bless you, Ere Zeta, bless you on your journey." A vivid image of Ere Zeta surrounded, filled, and protected by white Light appeared to me. My shoulders dropped and my body entered into a deep state of relaxation. I knew that there was nothing for me to do, nothing to fix or to change or to control. I opened my eyelids and said, "I just received a letter from him, Michael. When did he die?"

"Last week, June 27th."

"That's impossible, I... Michael, hold a minute," I said quickly and less distinctly. I reached for my pocketbook, groped around inside until I fished out the letter from Ere Zeta and said, *"It's dated July 2nd and postmarked July 3rd from London.*"

Michael chuckled then broke into laughter, which roused an explosion of laughter in me, which in turn provoked him into roaring and snorting. I laughed until my stomach and sides ached.

When the laughing subsided, he said, "Remember Ere Zeta telling us that laughter was a sure sign the spirit was present."

His voice cracked and we both began to weep. And then to laugh again. We were children, laughing and crying at the same time.

"Michael, I'd like to read the letter to you."

"Please," he said.

2nd July

Beloved Darjeeling,

I am with you in your heart and you have known this. It is time to know it in a greater way, for you stand on the threshold of entering into the high country. Whenever you need strength or love in a greater way turn to your heart. It is there. The love will come through you in your expression. Others will recognize this love and will be lifted and will know the greater reality.

In Light and Loving,

Ere Zeta

"Thanks for sharing that, Darjeeling. It touched me, opened my heart."

"My heart as well. I love you, Michael. I'll speak to you soon.

A month and a half later I was packing for a week long trip to visit my daughter in South Africa. The bungalow seemed stuffy. I opened the sliding glass door and walked out onto the small porch. As I leaned against the railing and looked at the vast expanse of sea before me I remembered the one who awakened me into the Light and the essence of my own divinity. Though Ere Zeta has passed back into the heart of God, his teachings live on inside of me, in my works, through my children, and I still see him occasionally...in my dreams, in the night travels, in the mystery school.

I looked across the sea toward Africa and I thought about my grandmother. How proud she'd be that I'm fluent in Swahili and even more so that I went in search of the river beneath the river and found out that its name is Love. I understood in that moment that it had been unnecessary for me to cross an ocean to find out who I am. Had I made it a priority and taken the time to look inside for that sacred place of peace, I would have come to know that I am the pure love of Spirit. Love that when it is aware of itself is afraid of nothing, wants nothing, is free.

Reading Group Discussion Questions

1. Despite poverty, loss, family secrets, shame, suffering and injustice, *The River Beneath The River* is an uplifting story. How does the author accomplish this?

2. What are your feelings about Darci's behavior. Are you challenged by her candid expression? Are there areas in your life where you can embrace freedom by suspending judgment?

3. Darci tells us that as a child she didn't fit in. Can you relate?

4. Discuss the relationship between Pini and Sela Beriman. What happens to children when they witness their parents' discord?

5. Were you surprised that Darci's childhood friend, Natalie did not resurface in the story? What do you think Susan's motives were?

6. What is the deeper significance of Darci becoming Darjeeling? Have you ever considered changing your name?

7. Through Ere Zeta and the mystery school, Darci connects with her own spirit. How might your life be transformed in knowing an enlightened being?

8. Discuss Darjeeling's path into motherhood. Examine what your place in the world is concerning people who are different than yourself.

9. What are the underlying themes of this story?

10. How does this novel make you look at your life differently than you did before? Discuss how you are more aware of the rivers that flow beneath the surface of your life.

About the Author

 Susan Tabin is an avid student of life. From her post-college days in the mid 1960's as a teacher in the New York City school system, to home schooling her two children in the 70's, to taking a year off from her endeavors to travel across the US with her family in a motor home, she has met life with a passion and a voracious appetite for learning. Susan lives with her husband in a lakeside home in southern Florida.